In the back room, Mr. Smock stepped into the walk-in cooler and powered up his shortwave radio.

Pondering what source to consult, Smock considered the fact that the Fountain of Youth's location was a deep dark secret. Not even his scientist pals, with whom he freely traded information, would know where it was.

He would have to consult the ultimate source of knowledge, the font of all wisdom, the keepers of even the most obscure yet vital facts in the universe. He dialed the frequency of the Milwaukee Public Library Ready Reference service and crossed his fingers....

STAR WRECK IV
Live Long and Profit
A PARODY

St. Martin's Paperbacks Titles by Leah Rewolinski

STAR WRECK IV

LIVE LONG AND PROFIT

A collection of cosmic capers
by

LEAH REWOLINSKI

ILLUSTRATIONS BY
HARRY TRUMBORE

A 2M COMMUNICATIONS LTD. PRODUCTION

ST. MARTIN'S PAPERBACKS

Published by arrangement with the author

STAR WRECK IV: LIVE LONG AND PROFIT

Copyright © 1993 by Leah Rewolinski.

Cover illustration by Bob Larkin.
Text illustrations copyright © 1993 by Harry Trumbore.

ISBN: 0-312-92985-4

Printed in the United States of America

St. Martin's Paperbacks edition/April 1993

10 9 8 7 6 5 4 3 2 1

To Gimli and Riley

Acknowledgment

Thanks to Tom for turning me on to "Star Trek: The Next Generation." That was five years and four books ago. Who'da thunk it?

Contents

The Return of the
Pink Slip

"**D**ARLING, WAKE UP. Jim, dear, it's morning." The voice of Counselor Deanna "Dee" Troit floated through Capt. James T. Smirk's sleeping quarters aboard his ship, the USS *Endocrine*.

Smirk turned over in bed, pulling the silk sheets over his head. Troit's voice continued to coax him gently. "The universe needs you. There are worlds to be explored and battles to be fought. Time to get up and buckle your swash."

Smirk rubbed his hands over his eyes. "Coming, darling," he mumbled. He sat up and pressed the "off" button of his alarm clock, silencing the recording of Troit's voice. *Too bad it's just an electronic reconstruction,* he thought. *But someday soon, she'll be my bride, and it'll be her voice waking me up in person. I hope.*

At the moment, however, Deanna wasn't even aboard his ship. She was in her usual spot on Capt. Jean-Lucy Ricardo's vessel—the other USS *Endocrine*—parked next to Smirk's ship in orbit of Starbase Flamingo.

Smirk was grateful that he no longer had to share a ship with Capt. Ricardo. Smirk and his crew now had the luxury of their own vessel, a working model of the *Endocrine* which their wrekkie fans had given them at the conclusion of their previous mission. Yet without Deanna around,

Smirk had found that this was a hollow triumph.

Smirk swung his feet over the side of the waterbed, then groaned, remembering what was on today's agenda: they had to UltraFax over to Starbase Flamingo for a meeting with Ricardo's crew and Admiral Nonsequitur. *Ecch*, Smirk thought. *I could be out in space obliterating an alien race or showing off my macho profile after a fistfight. Instead, we have to sit around jabbering at each other in a dull, dry, boring meeting.*

As Capt. Jean-Lucy Ricardo awoke in his quarters aboard the neighboring ship, he lay in bed for a few extra moments, savoring the thought of what was in store for them today: a meeting.

There would be discussions ... voting ... consideration of every angle ... endless rehashes. It would be splendid.

Admiral Nonsequitur hadn't given them a detailed agenda as Ricardo had hoped. In fact, he'd refused to tell them what the meeting was about. But even without any anticipatory paperwork to savor, Ricardo was excited.

Ricardo headed to his bathroom, opened the medicine cabinet and scanned his large collection of skull waxes. Since today would be such a special day, he decided to use the Number 2 wax for the extra shine he'd need to stand out during the meeting.

Later that morning, after both crews had finished their water aerobics classes and eaten breakfast, they UltraFaxed over to Starbase Flamingo.

Capt. Smirk perked up when he caught sight of Deanna Troit in the hallway to the meeting room. He pushed his way toward her as the crowd of crewmembers funneled through the doorway. Deftly Smirk slipped his arm around Troit's shoulders. "Lovely morning, Counselor," he purred.

Troit glared at him. Smirk contorted his face into an

expression of bruised bewilderment. "Was it something I said?" he pouted.

"Take your arm off me, Captain," Troit said evenly.

"Unnhh—shot down again. You've pierced me to the core." Smirk clutched his heart as if in pain. Then, lowering his voice so no one else would hear, he added, "I *have* been having some stabbing pains in my back lately, Deanna. You aren't still sticking pins into that voodoo doll with my picture on it, are you?"

Troit sighed. "No. I told you, I've gotten over that."

They halted in the doorway as the others filed past them into the meeting room. Smirk felt encouraged. At least Deanna hadn't yet taken his breath away with an elbow jab in the ribs like the last time he'd tried to put the moves on her. Eagerly, Smirk studied her face; it looked like she had more to say to him.

For once, he'd read her correctly. With an air of resignation, Troit said, "Captain, we need to talk."

After the last of the other crewmembers had shuffled into the meeting room, Troit and Smirk remained in the hallway. Troit shut the meeting room door so they could speak in private.

"Talk away, my sweet," Smirk crooned. "Your voice is music to my ears."

"Oh, really?" Her tone hovered around 0 degrees Centigrade. "Too bad that wasn't the case when we were engaged to be married. Or better yet, when you broke off our engagement."

"That was a dreadful mistake," Smirk admitted. "Simply a case of cold feet, my dear. But now I've seen the error of my ways. You're the only woman in the galaxy for me. I must have you."

Troit shook her head sadly. "I'm sorry, Jim, but I've thought about it a lot. It's not a simple matter of making up with each other. I've decided you're just not my type."

"Not your type?" Smirk echoed. He held out his palms

beseechingly as if posing for her inspection. "What's not to like?"

Troit groped for words. "You're just too . . . too . . . I don't know . . . arrogant, I guess. Like when you assume that just because you want me, I'm going to want you, too. Or like when you're conducting a mission—you never consult your crew like Captain Ricardo does. You just order everybody around because you think you know their jobs better than they do."

"Well, I do," Smirk retorted. "I'm always right, and in the end we always come out on top. What's wrong with that?"

Troit shrugged. "Sometimes it's more interesting to root for the underdog," she replied. "You can't tell someone's character until they've really been tested."

"But I am being tested, my darling," Smirk said. "I have to prove myself worthy of your love. I've dedicated my life to that goal. Isn't that proof enough of my character?"

"No. Don't you see?" She began to slip into her counselor mode, her voice dripping with Profound Understanding. "You only want me because you can't have me. There are millions of women out there in the galaxy, but you focus on me simply because I'm unattainable."

Smirk felt a twinge of alarm. This wasn't going the way he'd planned. It was time to slather on an extra-thick layer of that old James T. Smirk charm.

"Can you blame me?" he whispered, putting on his best hurt-puppy expression. "Everyone else pales beside you. I am nothing without you, Deanna. I've given up all my hobbies to focus on our courtship. I hardly even watch TV anymore."

Smirk leaned closer, half-closing his eyelids as if overcome with longing. "Please come back to me. Please. Pleeeeeease." He closed his eyes completely and puckered his lips, tilting his head toward hers.

She regarded him with pity. "Get a life," she replied.

She doesn't mean it, Smirk told himself. *She's just*

"I've given up all my hobbies to focus on our courtship."

struggling to overcome her common sense. Any second now, she'll succumb. He leaned forward with his eyes still closed and his lips still puckered, unaware that Troit had left the hallway and gone into the meeting room without him.

Stay puckered, Smirk told himself. *Be ready.* His lips were starting to ache. *Gee, she's really taking a long time to come around.*

"Captain?" This came in a deep baritone. *Hmmmm,* Smirk thought, *either Deanna's voice has changed, or someone else is here in the hallway with us.* With lips outstretched, Smirk raised his eyelids slowly.

His right-hand man, Mr. Smock, stood there. Deanna was nowhere in sight. Mr. Smock gave an embarrassed little cough and continued, "Sir, the admiral has requested that you join us so we can begin the meeting."

Smirk retracted his lips. "The meeting. Ah, yes, the meeting." He straightened his tunic and headed toward the entrance. "Well, I guess these lip-toning exercises can wait. Have you ever tried them, Smock? They're much more practical than water aerobics when it comes to real-life applications."

They entered the meeting room, and Smirk sat down in the chair Smock had saved for him. Unfortunately, Smirk observed, it was nowhere near Deanna Troit; she was sitting halfway across the semicircle of chairs that faced the podium.

Smirk caught Troit's eye and silently mouthed "I love you" with exaggerated expressiveness. She frowned at him, then tossed back her hair and stared at the front of the room.

Admiral Nonsequitur stood at the podium, glaring at Smirk. "Glad you could join us, Captain," he began sarcastically. "The early bird makes the worm turn, eh?" Smirk gave him a conciliatory smile.

"But enough of this endless discussion," Nonsequitur went on. "Let's get down to brass taxes. Here's the bottom line: Financially, Starfreak is barely squeaking by.

"Naturally, we've tried all the standard remedies," Non-sequitur said, "like increasing the salaries of our board of directors, awarding bonuses to the executive staff, and investing heavily in remote outposts that we'll never use."

Something rustled at Deanna's elbow. The person next to her was handing her a note. She unfolded it and read:

Deanna and Jim up in a tree
K-I-S-S-I-N-G
First comes love, then comes marriage.
Let's find a wedding chapel in this parish.

Love,
Jim

P.S. I love you.

Troit crumpled the note, pointedly avoiding Smirk's eyes.

Admiral Nonsequitur continued, "None of these measures has helped. So we're going to resort to downsizing." A ripple of tension passed through the room. Suddenly everyone was listening intently. Even Capt. Smirk began paying attention.

"We can no longer afford to keep two identical ships in service, with duplicate staffs performing essentially the same functions," said Nonsequitur. "In fact, we can't even afford to keep you all on the payroll anymore. Therefore, we have decided..."

Nonsequitur glanced around the room and, sensing their animosity over this announcement, slipped into the passive voice. "...Uh, therefore, it has been decided that there will be just one USS *Endocrine,* and just one person in each staff position. We have decided—er, the decision has been made to utilize some members from each captain's crew. The rest of you will be temporarily laid off—er, outplaced."

Capt. Ricardo leaped to his feet. "Admiral, I object!"

"The ship Starfreak will keep in service," Nonsequitur went on, ignoring Ricardo's protest, "will be the one which Captain Ricardo's crew currently occupies, and he will be its captain."

"Oh, then, never mind," Ricardo said, sitting down again.

Several people glanced in Smirk's direction, expecting him to object in turn, but he was too stunned to say anything at all. Besides, he knew from experience that it was futile to protest; he'd been stripped of his command once before, and there was nothing you could do about it once the big shots made up their minds.

"Here are the other staff assignments," Nonsequitur continued. "Chief Bartender Guano will be promoted to first officer."

"What?!" screamed Commander Wilson Piker. "That's my job!"

"Correction: it *was* your job," Nonsequitur told him.

"But I'm supposed to be Number 1," Piker said. "What number am I now? Am I on the staff at all?"

Nonsequitur squinted at the list. "Piker . . . Piker . . . yes, here's your name. I'll get to your assignment in a minute."

"But—" Piker began.

Nonsequitur interrupted. "There will be no haggling over your assignments," he said. "Our team in Human Resources spent a lot of time determining exactly the right person for each of these jobs. And Starfreak will monitor your ship to make sure you *stay* in these jobs.

"Now," he continued, snapping his papers against the podium in annoyance, "if you'll all refrain from further outbursts, I'll read the rest of this assignment list, and then we can go for a swim in the pool. All right, here they are. Dr. McCaw will serve as second officer, and former Chief Engineer Mr. Snot will be communications officer.

"Ship's counselor is now Mr. Wart," Nonsequitur read. "Chief medical officer—that's you, Mr. Piker. Chief engineer, Deanna Troit."

Deanna looked as though she might faint. Smirk's heart went out to her. Then his heart returned to its customary self-centered position as he pondered whether he himself would make the team. If Starfreak gave him a new post, at least he and Deanna would serve on the same ship, which would vastly improve his courting potential.

Smirk prayed silently, *Please, let me have an assignment. Any assignment. Just let me make the cut.*

"Let's see, there are three positions left here," said Nonsequitur. "Security chief..."

Smirk, Smirk, Smirk, the captain thought, projecting his concentration toward the admiral.

"...Yoohoo," read Nonsequitur. "UltraFax chief..."

Smirk, Smirk, Smirk...

"...Checkout." Nonsequitur read the last line: "And chief bartender in the Ten-Foreplay lounge..."

Smirk, Smirk, Smirk, please let it be me, Smirk, Smirk...

"Mr. Smock. All right, people, you have your assignments. Now, everybody in the pool!" Nonsequitur slammed down his gavel to end the meeting. A buzz of discussion filled the room as everyone stood up and began reacting aloud to this stunning development.

Everyone, that is, except Capt. Smirk. He slumped in his chair, unable to believe his bad luck. *Shot down twice in one morning,* he thought, wincing.

On his way out, Capt. Ricardo gave Smirk a hearty pat on the shoulder. "Tough luck, old chap," Ricardo said, unable to completely suppress a note of gloating in his voice.

Ricardo's newly-chosen crewmembers left the room with him, eager to celebrate at the pool party. The remaining six crewmembers gathered morosely around Smirk, reflexively seeking his leadership even though he'd just lost his official standing in Starfreak.

"Captain," asked Dacron the android, "could you explain the meaning of our new status, 'laid off er outplaced'?"

Smirk could only stare at him, too miserable to reply.

"Make that just plain 'laid off,' Dacron," said former Chief Engineer Georgie LaForgery. "No use sugar-coating it."

"Well, we still have a ship, anyway," pointed out Mr. Zulu. Georgie looked dubious, but Zulu shrugged and added in a hopeful tone, "Starfreak didn't say we couldn't keep on using the wrekkies' working model."

"Yeah, but without Starfreak's supplies and financial backing, we're not going to get very far," Georgie pointed out.

Dacron was still puzzled over what had happened. "Precisely what is our status relative to Captain Ricardo's crew now that we are 'laid off'?" he inquired.

"We don't *have* any status, Dacron," said Westerly Flusher. For a long time Westerly had been away, enrolled in Starfreak Academy Film School, but just the week before he'd quit school in a protest over artistic censorship. His innate sense of good timing had brought him back to the *Endocrine* just before this layoff. "Captain Ricardo's crew has the approval of Starfreak and access to all its resources," Westerly said, "meaning there's none left for us."

"We're out of it," agreed Westerly's mother, Dr. Beverage Flusher, who was formerly Capt. Ricardo's chief medical officer.

"I see," said Dacron. "In effect, they are the Haves, and we are the Have-Nots."

Dacron's observation seemed to strike a chord within Capt. Smirk. He began to emerge from his daze. "The Have-Nots," Smirk said quietly. "So it's come to this, eh? All these years of service, and I don't even get a gold watch. They just kick me out the door."

"Sir, don't you still own shares in Starfreak?" Zulu asked. "I thought you had a controlling interest, in fact."

"I sold them," Smirk said. "The market was bullish, trading was at an all-time high, and I needed some cash for a motorboat. So I sold all my Starfreak preferred shares

Westerly had been away, enrolled in Starfreak
Academy Film School.

and cashed in my IRA besides. Financially, I'm no better off than any of you right now. Here we are, the Have-Nots." He sat there looking dejected, apparently content simply to mope with his head in his hands.

The others, waiting for someone to take charge, began to get a little nervous. Finally, Ricardo's former UltraFax Chief, Smiles O'Brine, ventured, "Uh, Captain, shall I UltraFax us onboard your ship?" Smirk nodded, so O'Brine pulled out his remote-control unit and Faxed them up to the Bridge of the alternate *Endocrine*. At least there they could mope in familiar surroundings.

2

Get Your Butts
in Gear

THE NEXT MORNING, the Haves took on their new roles
aboard Capt. Ricardo's *Endocrine*.

First Officer Guano sat at the center of the Bridge
in the chair formerly occupied by Cmdr. Piker. The day
before, when Admiral Nonsequitur had given her the pro-
motion, Guano had felt pure excitement. But now that she
was actually assuming this position, she realized that her
former job as chief bartender might not have completely
prepared her to be second in command of a starship.

Guano wondered if Cmdr. Piker had left behind some
sort of job manual. She opened the storage compartment
of the chair and peered inside. But all she found were a
few crumpled Big Mac wrappers and an illustrated children's book, *A Beginner's Guide to Outer Space Terms*.

At his Operations ("Oops") station in the forward section
of the Bridge, Dr. McCaw scowled at the console panel.
He realized he was supposed to run this thing, but none
of the control buttons or readouts made any sense. A faint
odor of crankcase oil lingered in the upholstery of the
chair, reminding him that Dacron had occupied this station before the layoff.

McCaw noticed Guano checking her storage compartment, so he did the same with his, but it yielded only the
current week's copy of *Soap Opera Digest*.

Capt. Ricardo emerged from the Crewmover, the *Endocrine*'s nifty elevator system, and strode to his captain's chair. "What's that noise?" he inquired.

Instantly Guano went on the defensive. She knew that as first officer, she was responsible for keeping the vessel running smoothly; she was supposed to stay on top of things at all times. How would Piker respond in this situation? As she pictured him standing there, a Piker-like reply popped to her lips. "What noise?"

"That beeping," said Ricardo. "Don't you hear it?"

"Yes, I hear it," said Guano, "but I didn't know it was anything out of the ordinary."

"Dr. McCaw?" Ricardo said, turning toward the Oops station.

McCaw shrugged. "It's not coming from my panel, so I wasn't going to worry about it," he said.

"Mmmm," said Capt. Ricardo. "Where *is* it coming from?"

No one answered. Finally, the feminine voice of the computer spoke up. "The beeping tone is coming from the communication panel of the Tactical station. The phone has been left off the hook."

Capt. Ricardo walked over to the station, which stood on the elevated platform directly in back of the senior officers' command chairs. "Where's Mr. Snot?" Ricardo asked. "He's supposed to be staffing this area."

"Montgomery Ward Snot is in the Conference Room . . ." said the computer. It paused for several beats, then added, ". . . napping."

"Napping, eh?" Ricardo said with a frown. "Number 1, go wake him up and get him in here."

Guano sat filing her nails. Ricardo stared at the back of her enormous hat and repeated, "Number 1!"

McCaw, swiveling to look back at Guano, hissed, "Pssst! He's talking to you, hat head."

"Wha—?" Startled, Guano dropped her nail file. "Uh, yes sir. Right away, Captain." She scrambled to the Conference Room door at the back of the Bridge.

By the time Guano awoke Mr. Snot and brought him
back to the Bridge, Capt. Ricardo had adjusted the Tactical
station's console. The status line now read "incoming
message."

"Open a 'hey, you' frequency and put the caller on the
Viewscreen, Mr. Snot," ordered Ricardo, striding over to
his command chair.

"Viewscreen...Viewscreen..." muttered Snot, trying
to make sense of the communication panel.

Ricardo watched the Viewscreen, waiting for an image
to appear, but nothing happened. He turned around and
inquired, "Mr. Snot?"

"Just a minute, Cap'n," Snot replied, flustered. "I've got
t' figure out all o' this rigamarole—all these buttons 'n'
things...it's a very technical matter..."

Guano, standing next to Snot, broke in, "Just press that
one that says 'Place Caller on Viewscreen.'" She reached
for the button, but Snot slapped her hand away.

"I'll do it m'self, woman!" Snot snarled, pressing the
button.

Guano punched him in the shoulder. "Watch it, you!"
she squealed. "I'm your superior officer, you know."

On the Viewscreen, Admiral Nonsequitur had appeared
as soon as Snot pressed the panel button. He now watched
the skirmish at the rear of the Bridge: Snot shoved Guano
aside, and Guano responded by pinching Snot's arm.

"Say, now, what's all the fighting about?" Nonsequitur
demanded. "Is it somebody's birthday?"

Capt. Ricardo turned around for a moment, growled
"Knock it off, you two," and turned back to the Viewscreen
with a broad smile. "What can we do for you, Admiral?"
asked Ricardo.

"Starfreak has an important order for your crew, Captain," said Nonsequitur. "It's a purchase order. No, wait,
that's not right. It's some kind of order, though. An order
of fries? Drat, now I've lost my train of thought."

Only his years of Starfreak discipline kept Capt. Ricardo from fidgeting as he faced the Viewscreen, listening to Nonsequitur ramble on.

The admiral groped around in the mounds of paper on his desk. "Some kind of order . . . the High Command faxed it to me a few hours ago . . ." he mumbled to himself. He rummaged through one desk drawer after another, then grabbed his wastebasket and overturned its contents onto the desktop. "Ah! Here it is," he exclaimed, pulling a sheet of paper out of the refuse. "Why is it always in the last place you look?"

Dr. McCaw muttered out of the side of his mouth, "Probably because you stop looking as soon as you find it."

"Well, I won't waste your valuable time reading this entire order to you," Nonsequitur continued. "Except, perhaps, for the first sentence, which says, 'Starfreak hereby orders the USS *Endocrine* under the command of Captain Jean-Lucy Ricardo to locate the Fountain of Youth.' And maybe this second sentence: 'Once located, the fountain is to be claimed for Starfreak.' And this third sentence is pretty important, too. It says, 'The fountain is known to have anti-aging properties, and its waters can be bottled and sold throughout the galaxy.'

"And also the fourth sentence: 'Profit from the sale of Fountain of Youth waters will be used to offset the huge after-tax losses of Starfreak for the second quarter of 44430.' And the fifth and sixth sentences: 'Intelligence reports indicate that the fountain is located somewhere in the Vivi Sector and that our enemies the Romanumens are also seeking its whereabouts. Allowing the Romanumens to reach the fountain first would deal a devastating blow to Starfreak.' And the seventh and final sentence, 'Therefore, it is the opinion of the High Command that the crewmembers of the USS *Endocrine* should get their butts in gear.'

"Well, Ricardo, you've got your work cut out for you," said Nonsequitur. "I'd be pretty anxious to find that fountain if I were you. Especially after the way the accountants were talking at last night's budget meeting . . . something about cost centers and line-item vetoes—or was it Fritos?—and how we can't afford even one *Endocrine* . . ." Nonsequitur's voice trailed off as he became distracted by the Lava Lite on his desk.

A worry line creased Capt. Ricardo's brow. "Precisely what did they say, Admiral?"

"Mmmm?" Nonsequitur murmured, tracing his finger along the Lava Lite's surface, following the path of a floating blob. He mused, "You know, if we replaced all of the incandescent light bulbs in Starfreak Headquarters with fluorescents, we might save enough on the electric bill to afford another snack vending machine. Nonsequitur out." His image disappeared from the Viewscreen.

Capt. Ricardo nibbled nervously on his thumbnail. "What do you suppose he meant by that reference to the budget?" he wondered aloud. "Will they take us out of commission if we don't find this fountain for them?"

Guano felt she should respond to this vague threat to the crew, but she didn't know what to say, so once again she tried to approximate what Piker would have done. She stood up, cocked her head and ordered, "Red Alert!" This triggered a warning sound, and red lights along the walls began blinking on and off.

Piker's voice came over the intercom from Sick Bay. "Captain?"

"Never mind, Number—er, Commander—um, Mr. Piker. There's no emergency," responded Capt. Ricardo, shooting a disdainful glance at Guano. He ordered the computer, "Cancel Red Alert."

"I wasn't asking about the Red Alert, sir," Piker's voice continued. "I wondered if you could spare Dr. McCaw for a few minutes. We had a patient come in here with severe bleeding from a leg wound, and the tourniquet I applied worked pretty well—"

"Tourniquet?" muttered Dr. McCaw.

"—But then one of the orderlies loosened the tourni-quet," Piker continued, "and the bleeding really got out of hand—"

"I'm sorry, Mr. Piker," the captain broke in, "but you know Starfreak's orders: everyone has to work at their assigned tasks. We're being monitored to make sure we comply. Besides, I need Dr. McCaw here on the Bridge. We've just begun a new mission."

"Well, if he can't come here and help us stop the bleed-ing," said Piker, "can he at least tell me where to find the mop?"

Dr. McCaw scowled. He barked at the intercom, "It's probably in the broom closet next to Dr. Flusher's office."

"Thanks," said Piker, signing off.

Capt. Ricardo told the Bridge crew, "Let's get to that fountain before we become the victims of a line-item veto, shall we? Ensign, set a course for the Vivi Sector. Engi-neering," continued the captain, speaking to the intercom, "we'll need maximum power."

"Yes, Captain," came Deanna Troit's voice. "I'm study-ing the Jargon Manual right now. I think I have a pretty good idea of how the engine works."

Mr. Snot, at the back of the Bridge, shuddered when he heard this.

"Engage," ordered Capt. Ricardo.

As Capt. Ricardo embarked upon his new mission, Capt. Smirk languished aboard his own ship.

Here I am, hiding out in the captain's Ready Room, thought Smirk as he sat on the sofa. *I used to be so contemptuous of Ricardo when he did this. But what's the point of staying on the Bridge if we're not going anywhere?* Smirk sighed and continued carving the coffee table with his penknife, drawing a heart around "JS & DT."

Although Smirk's Have-Not crewmembers had boarded his ship and gone to their usual stations, they had no duties to perform. Without Starfreak's blessing, there would be no missions to conduct. Even if they had decided to go galivanting out on their own, they knew that eventually the Dilithium Crystal Vanish chamber in the Engine Room would be running on "empty," and Starfreak wasn't going to give them a refill.

Beep-beep boop-boop went the door chime. "Come in," said Smirk.

Dacron entered. "Captain, there has been—" he began, then halted, startled by the sight of Smirk carving the coffee table.

"Yes, Lieutenant? What is it?" Smirk said without looking up.

Dacron swallowed nervously, then ventured, "Sir, I believe that is unauthorized use of Starfreak property."

Smirk chuckled, a bitter smile crossing his face. "Well, let them come and arrest me, then."

Dacron stared at the carving. "Does this ritual signify your love for Counselor Troit?"

"My *unrequited* love, Dacron," said Smirk, chipping away at the wood. "Something you wouldn't understand. Something even I don't understand."

Smirk paused and stared off into the distance for a moment, then added, "Come to think of it, my love has never been unrequited before. No woman could resist me. Until Deanna came along." He pulled a ballpoint pen out of his pocket and began darkening the heart outline. "What was it you wanted, Dacron?"

"Sir, I have discovered an interesting development involving the other ship," said Dacron. "I listened in on their latest exchange with Starfreak Command."

"Really? I thought you used to spend the morning watching soap operas," Smirk commented.

"All of the programs have been pre-empted today by the President's State of the Universe address," Dacron replied. "To stay busy, I was monitoring the communication channels of the other *Endocrine.* I learned that they have been given a mission to find the Fountain of Youth. The fountain

"My love has never been unrequited before. No woman could resist me."

is to be an essential source of revenue for Starfreak."

"So?" Smirk said idly, picking up his knife again and etching an arrow to pierce the heart.

"Starfreak Command is unsure of the exact whereabouts of the fountain," Dacron continued. "They know only that it is somewhere in the Vivi Sector. Apparently they are unaware of an article published in last month's *Astronomy* magazine which reported that an amateur telescope maker had pinpointed the fountain's location. It is in the Hydrant Quadrant."

"So?" Smirk repeated.

"Sir, since we have more precise knowledge of the fountain's location, we could get there first," Dacron pointed out. "Claiming control of the fountain would increase our bargaining power with Starfreak. Perhaps they would reinstate our crew to full-time status."

"Hmmm." Smirk set down his knife and considered this possibility. Then he crossed his arms and slumped back on the couch cushions. "Oh, I dunno. What's the point?" he whined. "Even if we did all that, I still wouldn't have Deanna. Without her, it hardly seems worth it."

Yet despite his discouraging words, Smirk seemed unable to dismiss the idea. "Although . . . if we got there first, Starfreak Command *would* have to deal with us," he mused. "They'd never be able to lay us off again.

"But how are we supposed to get there before Ricardo's team?" Smirk continued. "We're really at a disadvantage. Starfreak has left us in a lurch." He stood up and paced the room, growing more annoyed with every step.

"We're cut off from Starfreak supplies and fuel," Smirk complained, "we're understaffed, and we've lost our official standing in the federation." Angrily he kicked the wastebasket; it sailed through the air and bounded off the glass of the built-in aquarium, startling the kissing gouramis.

"It was just a suggestion, sir," Dacron said, looking wary.

"I *hate* feeling so . . . so . . . powerless!" Smirk raged. "It's so frustrating to be the underdog!" He picked up the candy dish from the coffee table and cocked his arm as if to throw it; then suddenly he stopped, his arm frozen in midair. "The underdog," he repeated softly.

Smirk slowly lowered the candy dish and set it back on the table. "The underdog—yes," he said to himself. "The odds against us are tremendous. She knows that. We'd be coming from behind."

"Sir?" Dacron inquired, trying to follow Smirk's line of thought.

"That would really impress her," Smirk continued. "There we'd be, valiantly struggling against the odds, and Deanna would see us charging in at the last minute to beat Starfreak's hand-picked crew. A come-from-behind victory! That would show her I've got the right stuff.

"Yeah! Let's do it!" Smirk yelled, raising his fist in a power salute. "Dacron, you're a genius!" Exuberantly Smirk grabbed Dacron by the shoulders and smacked his cheek with a big kiss. Then Smirk trotted out of the Ready Room onto the Bridge, eager to begin this new venture.

Dacron remained standing as he was when Smirk kissed him, wondering why every time he thought he'd figured out human emotions, someone threw him a curve ball.

"So is everybody clear on what we're doing in this new mission?" Smirk said a short time later as he concluded his explanation to the others in the Conference Room.

Westerly raised his hand. "What was that part about not getting there before Captain Ricardo's crew?" he asked. "If we know where to find the Fountain of Youth, why don't we head straight over there?"

"Tactical reasons," Smirk replied crisply. "It's too involved for me to explain. Let's just say that it's essential we go in at the last minute and snatch the victory out from under them. Now, Mr. LaForgery," Smirk continued, addressing his chief engineer, "can you come up with a way to get us there even though we barely have enough fuel to maintain impulse power?"

Georgie screwed up his face in concentration. "It'll be difficult," he mused, "but I think it's possible. Maybe if we digitize the structural integrity fields to match the Jiffy Tubes, then transwarp the hull deflectors over their maximum range"—his voice grew more and more enthusiastic as he realized the possibilities—"and reconfigure the thermostats in the nacelle, and then use Lime-A-Way on the hard water deposits in the maintenance room . . . Bingo!" Georgie snapped his fingers. With a grin, he concluded, "It'll work, all right."

"Could you translate that into English for us, Mr. LaForgery?" asked Capt. Smirk.

"Sure, Captain," Georgie responded. "We'll use most of our available fuel to travel to within a few hundred kilometers of Captain Ricardo's ship. After that, we'll just draft them. We should be pulled along in their wake."

"Won't they know we're following them?" Westerly asked.

Dacron chimed in, "Their sensors will be able to detect another ship at such close range."

"I guess it depends on who's manning their sensor array at the Tactical station," Capt. Smirk observed. "The person would have to be sharp enough to notice an anomaly on the radar. Who was assigned to that station? Does anyone remember who Nonsequitur named to the post?"

"It was Mr. Snot," Zulu recalled.

"Oh. Then we're safe," Smirk concluded.

Ten-Foreplaying
Around

GEORGIE'S TECHNIQUE OF drafting the other ship for propulsion worked so well that the Have-Nots could just sit back and enjoy the ride.

It was three days since they'd begun following Ricardo's vessel, and Ricardo's Haves seemed completely unaware of their presence. The Have-Nots felt secure that Communications Officer Snot wouldn't detect them on his radar screen, and Dacron secretly monitored all of the Haves' Bridge conversations to stay alert for any unexpected upsurges in crew intelligence.

So far, though, everything he'd heard indicated that Capt. Ricardo had his hands full simply trying to maintain order among his ill-suited officers. Ricardo was much too busy to notice that another starship was trailing them across the galaxy.

Dacron activated the audio recorder to keep track of further conversations on Ricardo's Bridge. He planned to monitor the recordings later; right now it was time to join the gang in the Ten-Foreplay lounge.

Before leaving the Bridge, Dacron pulled out a portable audiotape player, slipped the cordless headphone plugs into his ears, and flicked the switch. Instantly, the Devo tape he'd gotten from the ship's archives brought a sparkle to his yellow eyes. Capt. Smirk had given him the cassette

Ricardo was much too busy to notice that another
starship was trailing them across the galaxy.

player in the hope that listening to music would stifle Dacron's incessant babbling, and so far the tactic was working.

As he pushed open the swinging doors of Ten-Foreplay, Dacron was surprised to see that his crewmates were in an extremely merry mood.

From his experiences in Ten-Foreplay on Capt. Ricardo's ship, Dacron knew that the beverages served there usually had only a mildly intoxicating effect. In fact, everyone but Dacron could sober up at will because the drinks were made from simpahol, a synthetic alcohol substitute. This late–24th-century development was the culmination of years of research funded by MADD.

But here in Capt. Smirk's Ten-Foreplay, Dacron observed, the drinks were making the humans act positively giddy. He popped out his earplugs so he could listen in on the conversation, curious to learn why things seemed so different this time.

"Do it again!" UltraFax Chief Smiles O'Brine was saying. "Here, Zulu, do the ritual with my pretzels." O'Brine stood up, wobbling a little, and slid his bowl of three-ring pretzels down the bar to Zulu.

Zulu scooped the pretzels from the bowl and stacked them neatly, one on top of the other, till the pile was several inches high. The others giggled in anticipation. Dacron noticed that even Capt. Smirk, who stood behind the bar wearing a server's apron, seemed amused by Zulu's antics.

"The Zen pretzel ritual begins," said Zulu in a deliberately pretentious voice, and the others guffawed. "The karate master projects his consciousness into the pretzels. He becomes one with the pretzels." Zulu stared at the pile, bug-eyed, and his crewmates laughed harder. Dacron, puzzled by their euphoria, tried in vain to analyze this latest manifestation of the human sense of humor.

"The karate master pictures himself breaking through the awesome combined strength of the pretzels," Zulu continued. Bev Flusher was laughing so hard that she had to lean for support against Georgie, who was sitting on the barstool next to her. He, in turn, wiped tears of laughter from the gutters of his visor. Westerly Flusher took a gulp from his glass of milk and leaned in close to get a better look at Zulu.

Zulu raised his hand high in the air. "The karate master breaks through the pretzels!" he cried. With a lightning-quick motion, Zulu sliced the side of his hand through the pile. Pretzels flew in every direction.

The others shrieked with laughter. Westerly Flusher chortled abruptly, and milk poured out of his nose. Capt. Smirk, helpless with mirth, clutched his aching sides and almost lost his balance. He grabbed out blindly for support and accidentally pulled the soda tap; cola gushed out of it. The sight of this doubled the frenzy of everyone's laughing fit.

Several minutes later, their roars and shrieks finally subsided to chuckles and giggles. There were long, satisfied sighs as everyone got back their breath and started to pull themselves together.

"What a party!" Georgie exclaimed. "I never felt like this in *our* Ten-Foreplay."

Bev Flusher nodded in agreement. "These drinks really pack a wallop," she said. "Captain, you mix a mean cocktail. Have you stocked your bar with a different kind of simpahol?"

"Simpahol?" Smirk replied, straightening his uniform. "What's that?"

Meanwhile, aboard Capt. Ricardo's ship, the computer had just gone down, and Ricardo felt an inexplicable chill of fear along his spine.

He gripped the arms of his command chair and told himself there was nothing to worry about. He'd sent technicians to investigate the problem. They could usually repair a computer malfunction within a few minutes.

With a lightning-quick motion, Zulu sliced through the pile.

Meanwhile, all of the ship's backup systems were operating normally. So what was making him so nervous?

I must have a subliminal memory of some catastrophe that coincided with an earlier computer malfunction, he reasoned. But what could it have been? He closed his eyes and pressed a fist against his mouth, trying to resurrect the half-buried memory.

Ricardo willed himself into trancelike concentration, blocking out the routine noises of the ship. He barely heard the *swooosh* of the Crewmover doors opening to admit someone onto the Bridge. Thus, he was completely unprepared for the falsetto shriek that assaulted his ears a moment later.

"Oh, Jean-Lucyyyyyy!" trilled the voice. It was the kind of sound that would have raised the hairs on the back of Ricardo's head, if he'd had any.

It was the voice of Deanna Troit's mother, Woksauna Troit.

Ricardo reflexively jerked backward, curling his legs onto the chair seat beneath him in a defensive posture. Woksauna Troit advanced, arms outstretched.

"There you are, you darling captain!" exclaimed Woksauna. "My, don't you look *commanding* today!"

Ricardo smiled wanly. He wondered what kind of embarrassing atrocity she wanted from him now, and whether he would be able to weasel out of it. So far his track record with Woksauna hadn't been too good, but maybe this time he could forestall panic long enough to think of a convincing excuse.

"I'm so glad I found you," Woksauna continued, "because I need your help."

Here it comes, Ricardo thought. *Stay alert, man!* His breath quickened, and his senses became ultra-sharp, like those of a hunted animal.

"I need you to pose with me for a fashion layout," Woksauna went on.

Fashion! Ricardo willed himself not to faint.

"It's for the next edition of *Betavoid Bride* magazine," Woksauna said. Then, coyly, she added, "They'd like to picture a mature couple in traditional Betavoid wedding garb."

Forcing himself to maintain a near-normal tone of voice, Ricardo replied, "But Woksauna, I thought it was traditional for a Betavoid bridal couple to be nude at the ceremony."

"Exactly," Woksauna said with relish.

Ricardo's flight-or-fight bodily reaction kicked into high gear. This was the moment of truth. He needed to come up with an excuse that would do more than just buy him time; it had to make Woksauna forget this absurd idea altogether. If he failed ... his mind raced: *Woksauna will drag me into the photo session ... I'll have to remove all my clothing ... and worse yet, I'll be forced to look at a naked Woksauna ... by Jove, the mere thought of it is enough to give one the hives ... the hives—that's it ... yes, I'll make up a story about that.*

Ricardo's vast relief lent an uncharacteristic sincerity to his smile. "I'm sure it would be a splendid opportunity," he told Woksauna, "and I'll make a point of taking you up on your invitation just as soon as my rash goes away."

Woksauna blinked. "Rash?"

"Yes," Ricardo replied brightly. "The worst of it is clearing up now—most of the scales have dropped off. Oh, I forgot," he interrupted himself. "You haven't seen it underneath my clothing. Would you like to have a look? I'm told it's almost past the contagious stage." He began lifting his tunic and reaching for her hand.

"Uh, no," Woksauna gasped. "No, thank you, Captain. Actually, I ought to get going." She backed away, keeping her eyes fixed on Ricardo's hand as he held it poised to lift his shirt. "I just remembered," Woksauna babbled, "that I, uh, left my ultrasonic denture cleaner plugged in." She backed into the railing that circled the center of the

Bridge, caught herself, turned around and fled to the Crewmover.

"Come on over to my quarters anytime," Ricardo called jauntily. "We can watch videotapes of the chemical peel treatments I underwent in Sick Bay." Woksauna summoned a queasy smile as the Crewmover doors closed.

Ricardo sat back in his command chair and savored his victory. But he had only a few minutes of peace. Apparently the computer was back on line, because its voice came over the intercom with another crisis for him to solve.

"Warning," the computer announced to the Bridge crew. "Unauthorized buildup of phaser energy on Deck 007."

"Security Chief Yoohoo," said Ricardo, hailing her over the intercom, "order your troops to investigate a phaser buildup on Deck 007."

"Sir—" Yoohoo answered instantly, then hesitated before continuing. "Uh, my troops are causing the buildup, sir."

"They're what?" Ricardo responded.

"They won't obey my orders," Yoohoo pouted. "They're upset about the compulsory Mary Kay makeover sessions I ordered for all Security personnel. Now these . . . these . . . troublemakers have set their phasers on 'stun,' and they've backed me into a corner."

"Are you trying to tell me you've got a mutiny on your hands?" Ricardo asked incredulously.

First Officer Guano, realizing that this presented a significant threat to the ship, jumped up and cried, "Red Alert!"

Capt. Ricardo scowled. "I hardly think this justifies a Red Alert, Number 1," he chided.

"Well, it's more important than a Yellow Alert," Guano said. "I mean, a Yellow Alert is practically meaningless." Capt. Ricardo gave her a cold stare.

Guano pressed her argument. "A Yellow Alert is like an amber traffic light," she said. "Nobody pays any attention to it." Ricardo's stony expression remained unchanged, but Guano continued, "We need something in between a Red Alert and a Yellow Alert." She cocked her head and ordered, "Cancel Red Alert. Begin. . . ." she searched her thoughts for a moment, then proclaimed, "Burnt Sienna Alert!"

Capt. Ricardo winced a little. It was much like the wince that Cmdr. Piker used to evoke from him, and in fact Guano was becoming more like his former first officer every day.

"Number 1," Ricardo said, "why don't you take a break? You've certainly earned it. Go down to Ten-Foreplay and relax for a while."

"You're sure, Captain?" Guano responded. "I wouldn't want to be away from my post when anything important happens."

"I'm sure we can manage," Ricardo said, trying to lift the corners of his mouth into a reassuring smile.

"OK," Guano agreed, "but be sure to call me the minute you see a crisis coming. Even a little one."

"We will, Commander," Ricardo said. As soon as Guano left in the Crewmover, Ricardo sighed with relief. Then, returning to the problem at hand, he spoke again to the intercom.

"Mr. Wart, we need your counseling services on Deck 007," said Ricardo, "to settle an argument among the Security troops."

"Yes, Captain," Wart's deep bass boomed in response.

This was followed a moment later by Piker's uncertain tone, hailing them from Sick Bay. "Uh, Captain?"

"What is it, Mr. Piker?"

"Sorry for the interruption, but I've got another question for Dr. McCaw," Piker said.

McCaw, who was sitting at his Oops console, frowned as he looked up at the intercom speaker in the ceiling. "Now what?"

"I'm about to perform an amputation," Piker said. "I

found Dr. Flusher's laser scalpel, but I can't figure out how to turn it on."

"Just flick the switch at the top of the hand grip," McCaw told him.

"I did, but nothing happens," Piker replied. "Nurse Ames," he continued, his voice fading slightly as if he were speaking to someone off to the side, "here, you try it." His voice returned to its normal volume as he said, "It's not just me. Nurse Ames can't get the switch to work, either."

"Then the safety catch is probably on," McCaw said. "It's located on the bottom of the tool."

"Where?" Piker asked. He continued, as if talking to himself, "Let's see, waveform amplitude—that's not it . . ."

McCaw warned him, "But before you release the safety catch, you have to clear the power setting you entered—"

"Ah, here's that safety catch," Piker went on.

A blood-curdling scream shot over the intercom from Sick Bay. In the background, someone cried out, "Nurse Ames! Oh, Cherry—your arm—oh, my gosh!"

"Oops," Piker said. "I guess it's working now. Thanks for your help."

Ricardo and McCaw stared at each other in disbelief. Then Ricardo shook his head as if to clear it. He brought up another matter. "Dr. McCaw, have you made any headway on figuring out how we can find the Fountain of Youth?"

"No, I haven't," McCaw responded. "Look, Jean-Lucy, what makes you think I can figure it out? I'm a doctor, not a tour guide. Now, if Mr. Smock were here—"

"But Mr. Smock is not here, Doctor," Ricardo cut in. "He is tending the bar in Ten-Foreplay, as Starfreak assigned him to do."

McCaw put on his most defiant I've-heard-this-all-before expression, but Ricardo continued.

"We're all under strict orders not to serve in any capacity other than those officially assigned," Ricardo nagged. "You know as well as I do that if I let Mr. Smock come here to

"Oops," Piker said. "I guess it's working now."

the Bridge and plot our course, as you've been insisting, Starfreak would yank our commission out from under us."

McCaw crossed his arms over his chest and began, "Well, if you weren't too proud to ask for directions—"

Ricardo cut him off. "Not another word out of you," Ricardo ordered, waving a reprimanding finger at McCaw. "I've had enough lip from you today. Do you understand?" McCaw glared at him, then swiveled back to his control panel without a word.

"And one more thing," Ricardo continued. "From now on you will refer to me as 'Captain' or 'Captain Ricardo', not 'Jean-Lucy' or 'chief' or 'boss.' " Ricardo tugged on his tunic to straighten it, as he often did out of habit, only this time the adrenaline rush from his anger made him pull so hard that he ripped the bodice seam. "Oh, for pity's sake," he muttered, going back to his command chair.

However, McCaw was determined to get in the last word, even if he was under orders not to speak. He began pressing the buttons of the Oops console out of sequence, attempting functions that he knew the console's software couldn't deliver. The panel emitted an annoying *zzst-zzst-zzst-zzst* with every attempt.

Ricardo ignored the tactic for a while, but when he felt a headache coming on he decided he'd had enough. "Dr. McCaw," he said, trying to keep his voice neutral, "perhaps you're due for a break also. Why don't you join Guano in Ten-Foreplay?"

"I don't like your Ten-Foreplay," McCaw responded. "The simpahol tastes like something from a kid's chemistry set." He kept poking the buttons. *Zzst-zzst-zzst-zzst.*

"That's an order, Dr. McCaw!" Ricardo declared, so McCaw was forced to drag himself onto the Crewmover.

The ensign sitting at the Conn station reported, "Captain, the engines can't maintain the cruising speed of Warped 3.14 you ordered."

Once again Capt. Ricardo spoke to the intercom. "Engineering," he said, "we're unable to maintain optimum power. What's wrong with the engines?"

Deanna Troit's voice answered him. "The engines are fine," she replied. "It's just that some of my crewmembers are still adjusting to their new jobs. Once they figure out what they're doing, we'll get up to full speed again."

"What do you mean, their new jobs?" Ricardo asked.

"Well, I sensed that many of them weren't happy with their usual assignments," Troit said. "They felt unfulfilled and discontented. So I let them trade jobs with each other. Psychologically, it's much more sound to have them doing work they enjoy. Once they're over this learning curve, things will be back to normal."

"Deanna," said Capt. Ricardo, rubbing his aching forehead with his fingertips, "this is not the time to have our Engineering crew learning on the job. Starfreak hasn't reassigned any of them the way they've done to our officers—thank goodness. I want you to return your crewmembers to their usual posts immediately."

"But Captain," Troit said, "I sense so much unhappiness here when they're doing work they don't like. There's a tremendous level of anguish, and as a Betavoid, I can't simply ignore it."

"Could you ignore it more easily if you weren't in Engineering?" Ricardo asked.

"I'm not sure," Troit said. "I'd have to be somewhere on the ship where there are contradictory emotions strong enough to mask what I feel here in Engineering."

"What about Ten-Foreplay?" Ricardo asked. "Everyone there is usually in a good mood."

"I suppose . . ." Troit conceded. "Yes, those positive emotions might be strong enough."

"Then make it so," Ricardo ordered. "Report to Ten-Foreplay, and stay there until further notice. *After* you get everybody back in their former jobs, that is."

"Yes, Captain," replied Troit, signing off.

Ricardo gazed around the Bridge. There was hardly anybody left. *Since the day shift began this morning,* he realized, *one by one I've sent all my Bridge officers to Ten-Foreplay.*

The sound of snoring at the back of the Bridge reminded Ricardo that this was not precisely true. *Well, I've sent away* almost *all of my Bridge officers,* Ricardo thought. *Mr. Snot is still at his post.*

Her work finished, Deanna Troit headed for Ten-Foreplay, as Capt. Ricardo had ordered. But the swinging doors to the bar didn't respond to her touch as usual. She pushed harder; they wouldn't budge.

Frowning, Deanna leaned on the door and pushed with all her might. It finally cracked open a few inches, revealing a mass of people on the other side.

As Deanna stuck her face into the opening, an ensign standing in the crowd with a drink in his hand asked, "Whaddaya want?"

"I'm just trying to get in," Deanna said.

The ensign made a sarcastic face. "Ricardo's already sent half the ship down here." Nevertheless, he pushed back the crowd to open the door a few more inches and yelled to those around him, "Hey! We got somebody comin' through!"

Twenty minutes later, panting and perspiring, Deanna finally squeezed through the last layer of patrons surrounding the bar. Dr. McCaw was sitting there, and he grunted when he saw her. "Ricardo sent you here, too, eh?" he asked. "I've never seen such a crackpot management method in my life. Anybody gets in his way, he sends 'em to the lounge. How did you people ever get anything done?"

"This isn't his usual style of command," Deanna sniffed. "He seems to be overreacting to stress just now. Perhaps he's hiding something, too." After receiving her drink order from acting bartender Mr. Smock, Deanna began elbowing her way back through the crowd, looking for a table.

"Hmmph," McCaw retorted, turning back toward the bar and redirecting his attention to Mr. Smock.

"Why aren't you smiling, Smock?" McCaw asked sarcastically. "Bartenders are supposed to smile and chat intimately with their customers. You know, draw them out. Make them feel good."

"I find it irrelevant to conduct small talk with patrons," Smock replied. "What logical purpose would it serve? No useful information is conveyed in such a conversation. As for my somber expression, it is a direct consequence of this post, for which I am drastically overqualified."

"You're telling me," McCaw groused. "I can't believe I went through med school and fifty-nine years of practice just to end up punching buttons on a Plexiglas panel at the front of the Bridge. Not to mention taking orders from somebody who couldn't tell a catheter from a stethoscope if his life depended on it."

McCaw swallowed his drink in a single gulp, then coughed and wheezed. "Arrtch! I wonder what this simpahol stuff does to your innards?" His crabbiness increased by several notches, and he scanned the room for another target.

Yoohoo sat on a nearby barstool. McCaw jerked his thumb toward her and told Smock, "Yoohoo's Security troops had her backed into a corner. Ricardo sent Wart to straighten things out. Well, Security Chief," McCaw taunted Yoohoo, "did *Counselor* Wart get you out of that tight spot?"

"As a matter of fact, he did," Yoohoo responded haughtily. "He took them all to his office for a counseling session." She pulled a makeup compact out of her purse and checked her reflection in its little mirror. Then, satisfied that none of her features had moved since she'd last checked, Yoohoo closed the compact and dropped it back in her purse.

"Hmmmph," grumbled McCaw, irritated that he hadn't gotten a rise out of Yoohoo. Noticing that Troit had found

"I find it irrelevant to conduct small talk with patrons," Smock replied.

a seat with Guano at a nearby table, McCaw called out, "Hey, Guano! You're with the wrong person. You should be seeing a hat shrink, not a headshrink."

Guano started to stand, rolling up her sleeves as if preparing for a fistfight, but Troit held her back. "Just ignore it," Troit said. "You don't want to encourage him."

"Yes, I do," Guano replied. "I want to encourage him, and I want to aggravate him, and then I want to take him out back and break his nose." But Troit firmly gripped Guano's sleeve and pulled her back into her chair.

Yoohoo left the bar and joined them at their table. "He's just a blowhard," Yoohoo told Guano. "Don't give his malarkey the dignity of a reply."

"That's right," Troit agreed. "Let's talk about something more pleasant. Like sex, for instance."

"Hmmm. That reminds me, Deanna," Guano said. "Your mother dropped in on the Bridge this morning."

Troit's smile faded into a look of exasperation. "I suppose she came on to Captain Ricardo again?" Troit asked. Guano nodded.

"She did *what?*" Yoohoo gasped.

Guano explained to Yoohoo, "Deanna's mother goes into heat every so often. It's some kind of Betavoid change-of-life thing. Whenever that happens, she comes on board. Her ultimate goal is to finagle a weekend at Club Bed with the captain."

"Does she ever succeed?" asked Yoohoo, sipping her drink.

"No," said Deanna. "I think Captain Ricardo is afraid of her. He prefers the old-fashioned type of woman—you know, one with a regular menopause like Mom used to have."

"I wish I could have seen that," Yoohoo said. "When did it happen?"

"Early," Guano told her, "while the computer was down." She turned thoughtful. "You know, it's funny that the computer was down during Woksauna's visit," Guano mused, "because the computer was down the *last* time she was on board, too. That was before we got our new job assignments. I remember it distinctly because her valet, Lurch, ordered special drinks for the two of them here in Ten-Foreplay. I tried to call up the directions, and the computer voice wouldn't respond."

Deanna shrugged. "It's probably just a coincidence," she said.

But Guano pursued the idea. "Come to think of it," she went on, "I've never seen the two of them operating simultaneously. Woksauna Troit and the computer, I mean. It's sort of like Clark Kent and Superman, you know?" Sensing their apathy, Guano asked her companions, "Doesn't it make you the least bit curious?"

"Not really," said Deanna, stirring her drink with a swizzle stick. "I already know more about my mother than I want to know."

Back at the bar, McCaw was still cranky, and he searched for a new victim. Checkout sat a few barstools away, nursing a beer. McCaw called to him, "Might as well make yourself comfortable there, Pavlov."

Checkout looked up blearily, and McCaw continued, "You won't be needed to UltraFax anybody down to the Fountain of Youth, 'cause at the rate Ricardo's going, we'll never find it. Har har har."

At that moment Capt. Ricardo's voice came over the intercom. "Attention, all officers," he said. "Report to your stations. We have arrived at Planet Stradivarius—9 and will now investigate the Fountain of Youth."

Disbelief and annoyance fought for dominance in McCaw's expression. "Well, I'll be hornswoggled," he crabbed.

4

The Look
of Love

"**A**ND FOR THOSE who think it's
necessary to consult maps or
rely on others for directions,
let this be a lesson to you," said Capt. Ricardo, winding
up his lecture to the Bridge crew. "An accomplished ex-
plorer can navigate by the stars. It's a simple matter of
knowing your constellations."

The Haves were now back on their Bridge, with everybody standing by to contact the planet Ricardo had found;
even Mr. Snot was awake and alert.

"They're hailing us, Cap'n," Snot reported from his Tactical station.

"Put them on the Viewscreen, Mr. Snot," said Ricardo.

As soon as Snot switched on the "hey, you" frequency,
the opening of a motion picture burst onto the Viewscreen.
Its achingly bright shot of a tourist resort was backed with
a lush musical soundtrack.

"Welcome to Stradivarius—9, playground of the galaxy,"
said an announcer. The film's visual image switched to a
fur-covered platform bed in the middle of a gaudy hotel
room. The announcer intoned, "We invite you sit back,
relax, and enjoy your stay. We have accommodations to
suit every taste and budget.

"While you're here, be sure to visit our Lover's Lounge,

where our renowned chef, Pierre Dupa, serves up his glorious four-star cuisine," the announcer continued. On-screen, Chef Pierre stood at tableside displaying a flaming Baked Alaska to an appreciative couple and then dousing the flames with a fire extinguisher.

"What the devil is this?" McCaw wanted to know.

"But of course, the main attraction is our famous fountain," the announcer continued. The screen showed swimsuit-clad tourists frolicking in the dancing waters of a fountain that dominated an outdoor courtyard. "No visit would be complete without a dip in the fountain. You'll feel frisky as honeymooners!" The location coordinates of the fountain were superimposed on the screen.

"That must be it," Ricardo concluded. "Dr. McCaw, relay those coordinates to Mr. Checkout in Shipping and Receiving. We'll send an Away Team down there immediately to claim the fountain for Starfreak."

"Claim it for Starfreak?" McCaw said. "What about the people who are already here? They've got quite a resort operation going. Won't they be a little upset if we try to claim it?"

"Hmmm. You're right, Doctor," Ricardo replied. "They may indeed put up a fuss. Mr. Snot, arm the futon torpedoes, just in case."

"Aye, Cap'n," Snot replied, pressing the appropriate buttons on the "anti-communication" section of his communication panel.

"There's something funny about all this," McCaw went on. "I thought the Fountain of Youth was supposed to be the best-kept secret in the galaxy. This place looks more like Disney World."

"Never mind, Doctor," Ricardo said. "Just relay the coordinates to Shipping. Number 1," Ricardo continued, turning to Guano, "you'll lead an Away Team down to the fountain. You'd better take some Security personnel along in case you meet with resistance." Guano nodded in reply.

"Counselor Wart," Ricardo said to the intercom, "have

you finished with the Security personnel yet?"

"We are in the semi-final rounds, Captain," Wart's voice replied. "We're down to the final four survivors."

"What?!" Ricardo yelped. "You're supposed to be conducting a counseling session, Mr. Wart."

"You asked me to settle their dispute, Captain," Wart replied. "In addition to their quarrel with Security Chief Yoohoo, they had internal disagreements, so I am holding elimination rounds here in my counseling office. In keeping with Kringle ritual, each combatant uses the weapon of their choice. It is a highly efficient method."

Ricardo, looking dizzy, leaned against his command chair. "How many of these Security people did you say are left, Mr. Wart?" he asked weakly.

"Four. And each one is a hardy warrior," Wart asserted.

"Yes, I'm sure they are," Ricardo said with a dazed look. "Well, I think you ought to end the contest now, Mr. Wart. Declare them all the winners."

"As you wish, Captain." Wart signed off.

Ricardo stared off into the distance. Guano waited several moments, then prompted him, "Uh, sir, you wanted me to lead an Away Team. Should I take those four Security people with me?"

Ricardo gazed blankly at Guano for a moment, then shook himself back into alertness. "Uh . . . no—not them," he said. "Choose your own Away Team, Commander."

"Yes *sir!*" Guano answered enthusiastically. She mused aloud, "Let's see, who should I take?" An Away Team mission would be a plum assignment, since all the crewmembers were itching to get off the ship for a change of scenery, and this Stradivarian resort looked especially promising.

Guano turned around slowly to survey the Bridge, resting her gaze on several crewmembers in turn as if considering and then rejecting them. "Dr. McCaw? Nahh. Ensign Roach? Uh-uh. Mr. Snot? Mmmm . . . nope."

Abruptly, Guano swiveled toward the front of the Bridge and said to the intercom, "Deanna Troit and Mr. Smock,

"In keeping with Kringle ritual, each combatant uses
the weapon of their choice."

report to Shipping and Receiving for an Away Team assignment." Then she strode off toward the Crewmover, leaving crewmembers scowling in her wake.

Guano had never really considered taking along anyone from the Bridge crew. Earlier, when she realized that as first officer she might someday get to lead an Away Team, she'd decided to take along Troit, who was her best friend, and Smock, who could provide the necessary brainpower.

The three of them converged on Shipping and Receiving, where UltraFax Chief Checkout was frantically trying to decipher his UltraFax control panel.

On board the Bridge of the Have-Nots' ship, which lurked around the corner behind an asteroid, Capt. Smirk asked Dacron, "What are they up to, Lieutenant?"

"Captain Ricardo's crew is orbiting a planet known as Stradivarius–9," Dacron reported. "This resort planet is famed for its Fountain of Love, which evokes strong feelings of affection in anyone who touches, swims in, drinks, or fills water balloons with its liquid."

"Ha! They're lost," Smirk concluded. "They probably think that's the Fountain of Youth."

"Captain, sensors indicate that they are powering up their UltraFax," Dacron observed. "They may be preparing to send an Away Team down to the surface."

"We'd better keep an eye on them. We might find out something useful," Smirk said, thinking, *Maybe they'll take samples of that water back to the ship. What if Deanna drinks some of it eventually? I want to be nearby if she starts feeling affectionate.*

"We'll send an Away Team, too," Smirk decided aloud. "Mr. Dacron, I want you and Beverage Flusher to beam down there. You'll be less conspicuous if you go as a couple. From a distance, you might even be mistaken for honeymooners. Stay out of sight of Ricardo's team, and report to me anything they do."

"Aye, sir," said Dacron, leaving the Bridge.

A few minutes later, as Dacron and Bev stood on the UltraFax platform, Capt. Smirk's voice came over the intercom with an update for UltraFax Chief O'Brine. "Mr. O'Brine, it sounds like Ricardo plans to Fax his Away Team right next to the Fountain of Love," Smirk said. "Wait till your sensors tell you they've begun Faxing, and then put our team somewhere nearby."

"Yes, Captain," O'Brine said, setting the panel controls.

Back on Ricardo's ship, Guano, Troit and Smock waited nervously on their UltraFax platform, wondering if Checkout could handle the delicate machinery that would disassemble them into itty-bitty molecules and reassemble them on Stradivarius–9.

Checkout's anxious expression as he surveyed his control panel was not reassuring. "I tink I've got it set up right," he said dubiously. "Everybody ready?"

Guano and Troit shrugged. Smock responded, "Energize, Mr. Checkout."

"Here you go," Checkout said, waving his hand across the activation sensor.

The three of them felt the familiar UltraFax tingle, that tickly sensation of showering in ginger ale. Then they rematerialized—but not on Stradivarius–9. Gazing around them, they saw that they were indoors somewhere.

"That's not the fountain, is it?" Troit asked innocently, pointing at a white porcelain structure in which Guano had landed. Water emerged from an outlet near the top of the fixture, washing down its surface and gurgling into a drain at floor level.

Smock's face reddened. "No, it is not," he replied. "That is a urinal."

"Aaakkk!" cried Guano, leaping out of it.

Smock continued, "It seems Mr. Checkout has beamed us into the men's room." The blush spread from Smock's face to the pointy tips of his ears, turning them a brilliant shade of magenta.

"That's not the fountain, is it?" Troit asked innocently.

"You mean we're still on the *Endocrine?*" Troit said with dismay.

"Aakk! Ecchh! Yukkk!" Guano cried, vigorously wiping off her feet against the floor tiles.

As Checkout's control panel revealed his mistake to him, he reset the UltraFax and tried again. The three Away Team members felt themselves phasing away from the men's room.

Meanwhile, the activation of Checkout's UltraFax had triggered sensors in O'Brine's UltraFax, setting off the automatic response that would beam Dacron and Bev down to the fountain.

O'Brine had also programmed a slight delay into his UltraFax, offsetting his Away Team's arrival to avoid a collision with the Haves. But since O'Brine hadn't anticipated the Haves' detour to the men's room, suddenly both Away Teams were traveling toward exactly the same coordinates at exactly the same instant.

Guano, Troit and Bev materialized normally, side by side. "What are *you* doing here?" Troit asked Bev.

But before she could answer, they were distracted by the sight of the two remaining UltraFax beams becoming crossed with each other at the edge of the Fountain of Love. As Dacron and Smock materialized on the same spot, the impact sent them both reeling. They teetered for an instant on the fountain's edge, then fell in.

Troit and Bev rushed to help them. "Are you all right, Dacron?" Troit asked, reaching for his arm.

Troit noticed that Dacron looked different. It wasn't just that his uniform was soaked and his hair was dripping. There was something in his expression that she'd never seen before. If it had been anyone but Dacron, Troit would have identified it as the look of love.

His eyes were dreamy as he clasped her hand. "I am fine, Counselor," he said. "In fact, I feel wonderful." He climbed out of the fountain and stood next to her wit. syrupy smile on his face. "It was so kind of you to come to my assistance," Dacron said. "You have earned my eternal devotion."

Troit felt puzzled. Dacron wore the look of love, all right. It was on his face. It was the kind of look that time can't erase. But how could this be? Dacron was an android, and Troit knew that androids could not feel emotion—a fact that Dacron had pointed out to the crew several times a day for the past five years. Yet her Betavoid telepathy told her that he did, indeed, feel love for her.

Standing next to them, Bev helped Smock step out of the fountain. "Oh, Mr. Smock, you're drenched," she observed.

"But it shall not quench my passion," Smock replied, holding her hand gently.

"Huh?" Bev responded.

"Thou art wonderful, Beverage," Smock declared. "As beautiful as the moons of Mebzorp." He kissed her hand.

Startled, Bev pulled her hand away and took a step backward. She glanced at the others and noticed Dacron's lovesick expression. "Uh-oh," Bev said, looking back and forth between Dacron and Smock. "I think I see what's going on here."

"What *is* going on?" Troit asked.

"They fell into the Fountain of Love," said Bev. "It gave them a strong dose of free-floating affection. You and I were the first ones they laid eyes on, so we've become their love objects."

"The Fountain of Love?" said Troit. "Captain Ricardo said we were beaming down to the Fountain of Youth."

Bev shook her head. "You're not even close," she confided.

Nearby, Guano was filling bottles with water from the fountain and stashing them in her hat.

er, "Guano, let's go. This isn't the right
to get back to the ship."

n a sec," Guano requested. "I want to stock-
this stuff in case I ever get back my old
job. It'd sell like hotcakes in Ten-Foreplay."

5

Sorta
Suitors

"**Y**OU SAW DACRON and Beverage Flusher?" Ricardo repeated. "Arriving together at this . . . Fountain of Love? What were they doing there?" He paced the Ready Room, where he was debriefing Guano after her Away Team returned from Stradivarius–9.

Guano shook her head. "I'm not sure. Maybe Bev is getting desperate. Her husband's been dead quite a while now, you know."

Ricardo didn't hear her; he was caught up in the possible implications of this sighting. "How did they get here?" he said to himself. "When we left, they were all stuck on Starbase Flamingo. And why would they arrive at the same time we do? I wonder if Smirk is behind this. Could he be piloting his ship around here somewhere?"

Ricardo started to head back to the Bridge, intending to order Mr. Snot to do a sensor scan of the area; then he stopped and turned back toward Guano. "Commander," he said, "is there anything else that happened on your away mission that I should know about?"

Guano recalled the bizarre phenomenon of Smock falling in love with Beverage after being drenched by the fountain. Surely Capt. Ricardo would want to know that his Vulture bartender had gone bonkers. But she feared that if she described the effects of the fountain water,

Ricardo would start asking around and eventually find out about the stockpile of bottles in her hat. The captain would probably force her to turn her Fountain of Love water over to Starfreak.

"Nope. It was just your typical away mission," Guano replied breezily, as if this hadn't been the first away mission of her life.

As Capt. Ricardo stepped back onto the Bridge, Mr. Snot told him, "Cap'n, we've got a message comin' in from Starfreak Headquarters."

"Onscreen, Mr. Snot," Ricardo said, turning to face the Viewscreen.

Admiral Nonsequitur appeared on the screen. "Ricardo, this is Admiral Nonsequitur calling," he said.

"I know, Admiral. I can see your face," Ricardo reminded him.

"Oh," said Nonsequitur. "Huh. Maybe I should have shaved this morning." He began rummaging distractedly through the clutter on his desk, picking up pencils that were scattered among the heaps of paper.

As Ricardo waited, Nonsequitur pulled out an electric pencil sharpener and set the pile of pencils to the left of it. He inserted pencils into the sharpener one by one, laying each pencil neatly to the right of the sharpener when it was finished. Then he picked up the entire pile, placed it on the left again, and began re-sharpening the pencils.

Ricardo cleared his throat. "Uh—Admiral . . . ?"

Nonsequitur looked up. "Ah, Ricardo! I'm glad you called," he said.

Just then, as if someone had thrown a switch, an uncharacteristic look of alertness dawned in Nonsequitur's eyes. Ricardo, having seen this happen before, perked up and waited for Nonsequitur to say something worth hearing.

"I have an important message for you," Nonsequitur said. "One of our scout ships reported seeing a Romanumen wartbird—their flagship vessel, the *Brassiere*—undoubtedly heading for the Fountain of Youth. However, they're going in the opposite direction from where your ship is headed."

Ricardo fidgeted in embarrassment.

"Meanwhile, you people are screwing around in orbit of this . . . this . . . Love Planet," Nonsequitur went on. "If you're that lonely, Jean-Lucy, why don't you call one of those 900 numbers that lets you have a long conversation with a menopausal Betavoid?"

Ricardo wondered why Nonsequitur's rare moments of mental clarity always seemed to coincide with a screwup by his crew. This was worse than the time Nonsequitur unexpectedly called them during that unauthorized Earl Grape Tea Party, during which Ricardo had allowed an ad agency to film a commercial on his Bridge in exchange for six cases of tea.

"We'll get right on it, Admiral," Ricardo promised.

"You do that," Nonsequitur affirmed, "or else both your crew and Captain Smirk's will go on permanent layoff."

Ricardo nervously nibbled his thumbnail as Nonsequitur went on. "The expenses of both *Endocrine*s will be charged against income from the Fountain of Youth, once we find it," Nonsequitur said. "I just came back from a meeting with the accountants, and they made it quite clear: no fountain, no *Endocrine*s."

Then, as mysteriously as it had arrived, the clarity began to fade from Nonsequitur's eyes. He stuck a ballpoint pen into the sharpener and frowned as he listened to the blades grinding against plastic. He looked up and asked, "Have I ever told you about my years at Starfreak Academy?"

"No, Admiral," Ricardo said, feigning interest.

"Good!" Nonsequitur barked. "Because that's none of your business!" He flicked off his transmission and disappeared from the Viewscreen.

Capt. Ricardo sighed. He turned toward Ensign Roach Blarin' at the Conn station and ordered, "Ensign, lay in a course to follow the *Brassiere*. And set our cruising speed at Warped 6.7."

"Sir, what coordinates shall I enter?" asked Ensign Roach. A series of wrinkles furrowed the bridge of her nose, as was characteristic of her humanoid species, the Bridgeorans.

Roach continued, "The admiral said the Romanumens are headed in the opposite direction from us, but right now we're not going in any direction, so what's the opposite?" Roach's puzzled expression created a new wrinkle in her nose.

"Ah. That is a problem, Ensign," Ricardo agreed. "We'll just have to continue to steer by the constellations."

"Which one, sir?" Roach responded.

"Read me the list again, will you?" said Ricardo, settling down into his command chair.

Roach pulled out her *Rand McNally Road Atlas and Star Chart* and consulted a map. "In this quadrant we have Phoenix the City," she read, "Orion the Studio, Mensa the Genius, Lynx the Car..."

"Oh, never mind," Ricardo interrupted. "Let's just follow that bright one over there." He pointed at the Viewscreen.

Roach squinted out into space. "Sir, that's a searchlight for the grand opening of a frozen yogurt shop."

"I know that," Ricardo retorted. "Follow it anyway."

By the time Capt. Ricardo remembered to check his sensors for the possible presence of Smirk's ship, the sensors showed that the Haves were alone. Unknowingly, by increasing Warped speed to 6.7, they'd left the others far behind.

On Smirk's ship, Chief Engineer Georgie LaForgery explained this new predicament to Smirk and Dacron as they met in the Ready Room.

"Captain Ricardo's crew took off too fast. They left us flatfooted," Georgie admitted. "We might be able to catch up and begin drafting them again, but getting to that point will really strain our reserves of Dilithium Crystal Vanish."

"Keep at it," Smirk urged him. "At least get us close enough so we can monitor their transmissions again. We have to stay up to date on what's happening with Dea—uh . . . that is, with any developments that might occur. Like this permanent layoff that Nonsequitur mentioned."

Georgie nodded and headed for the door.

"And, Mr. LaForgery . . ." Smirk continued. Georgie stopped and turned around.

" . . . Keep up the good work," Smirk added. "This is the first time in my career that I've had a chief engineer who can explain what he's doing." Georgie smiled, saluted, and headed back to Engineering.

Turning to Dacron, Smirk saw that the android still had that odd expression on his face, the Mona Lisa smile he'd worn ever since returning from Stradivarius–9. Then Smirk noticed the cordless earphone plugs that were jammed into Dacron's ears; Dacron had been listening to his cassette player and hadn't heard a word of their conversation so far.

Smirk reached over and popped an earphone plug out of Dacron's ear socket, startling Dacron into attention. Smirk held the plug to his own ear. "What are you listening to, Dacron?" Smirk asked curiously.

"Barry Manilow, sir."

"Barry Manilow? I didn't think your tastes extended to the sentimental, Dacron."

"Lately I have begun studying the computer's archives of human love songs and poetry, sir." Dacron didn't specify that "lately" meant just in the previous three hours since he'd fallen into the Fountain of Love. Before Smirk could question him further and discover that his first officer now had an enormous crush on the woman Smirk sought for himself, Dacron hastened to suggest the plan he'd concocted.

"Captain, I would like to try creating some of this literature myself," Dacron said. "Perhaps I could write poetry and love letters on your behalf. We could send them to Deanna Troit to test the feminine reaction to my work."

Smirk seemed amused. "You want to ghostwrite love letters for me?" he asked. He thought it over for a moment, then said, "Well, why not? Maybe your research will come up with some phrases that'll win her heart. Sure, Dacron, go ahead. Just let me see what you write before you send out anything with my name on it, will you?"

"Of course, Captain," Dacron replied.

"Also," Smirk added, warming up to the idea, "in your letters to her, be sure to emphasize our dire straits. I want to evoke Deanna's sympathy. Mention that we're low on fuel and trying our darndest to keep up. Make it sound like a valiant quest. Like we're down but not out."

"Yes, sir." Dacron stood up, preparing to leave.

"Oh, and Dacron," said Smirk, "try to make this material sound like I wrote it, all right? I know that may be difficult for you since you're an android without emotions, but these letters have got to seem authentic." Smirk draped a fatherly arm across Dacron's shoulders to ready him for a little pep talk. "When you're writing them, try to put yourself in my place."

Smirk's voice dropped to an evocative whisper. "There's this intelligent, beautiful, desirable woman. You'd give anything to have her." A faint pinkish blush spread across Dacron's chalky white cheeks.

"She is the peak of perfection," Smirk crooned. "Just thinking of her face ... her eyes ... her hair ... makes you tingle inside." Dacron began to breathe heavily.

"True union—physical, mental, emotional—would bring both you and this lovely creature to the peak of ecstasy," Smirk went on. Beads of sweat appeared on Dacron's brow.

"Well, Dacron," Smirk concluded, "do you get my drift?"

"Yes, Captain," Dacron replied. "May I be excused now, sir? I believe I need to take a cold shower."

"Ha ha!" Smirk slapped him on the back. "That's the spirit."

Several days later, Mr. Smock crept into the walk-in cooler in the back room of Ten-Foreplay on Ricardo's ship, making sure no one saw him enter.

Smock powered up the short-wave radio transmitter he'd secretly built in his spare time. He had rigged together this piece of unauthorized equipment from egg cartons, cocktail napkins, and other odds and ends scavenged from the bar. Now he would use it to try to contact Beverage Flusher. He hoped Smirk's ship had pulled into communication range once again so he could reach her.

He was in luck; his radio triggered Beverage's office phone. After two rings, she answered: "Beverage Flusher."

Smock nearly swooned when he heard her voice. Unaware that he'd contracted pneumonia after falling into the Fountain of Love, he knew only that the fever which had gripped his body all morning burned even hotter the moment Beverage spoke. His heart beat wildly, the way it used to when he heard a particularly logical theorem. "Dr. Flusher? This is Mr. Smock."

"Oh, hello, Mr. Smock." Her tone was friendly yet noncommittal. "What can I do for you today?"

Be mine, Smock almost blurted out. But he held back, recalling how startled Beverage had seemed when he'd climbed out of the Fountain of Love with words of flattery pouring from his lips. *I must avoid coming on too strong,* he thought.

Smock struggled to keep his voice calm. "There is a particularly interesting article in the latest issue of *Scientific American,*" he said. "I was wondering if you'd seen it. It concerns the entropy of the titanium isotope across the impedance of krypton nuclei." He struggled to catch his breath; his pneumonia-stricken chest grew tighter by the second.

"Yes, I did see it," Beverage replied enthusiastically.

"But what a radical notion they're proposing—that the frakesonian spineroscopy technique can be fragmented across the sirtis and mcfadden modes."

Smock coughed, caught his breath, then coughed again. "But that must be considered—" he broke off as another deep cough shook his chest and then subsided—"in light of the burton-wave theory, given the inevitable inaccuracies of the dornscope and the stewartometer in detecting goldberg variations."

"So true," Bev said with a sigh. She added, "You know, Mr. Smock, it's really nice to talk shop with a fellow scientist again. It gets so *lonely* around here sometimes."

The implied invitation in Bev's tone of voice made Smock draw in his breath sharply. This triggered another coughing seizure which gripped him until he could scarcely breathe.

Bev went on, "Maybe you could come over some evening. I'll make dinner, and we can have a cozy little chat by the light of the Bunsen burners."

Smock couldn't shake his fit of coughing. Struggling to draw in another breath, he felt himself blacking out.

"Mr. Smock?" he heard Bev ask. "Would you like that?"

Smock began seeing stars.

"Mr. Smock? Mr. Smock?" came Bev's voice from the radio transmitter. As he lost consciousness, Smock heard her pout, "Hmmph. Typical modern man. Show the least bit of interest and he flakes out on you."

Smock awoke on the floor of the walk-in cooler several hours later. His limbs were thoroughly chilled, yet his head burned with fever. Spasms of coughing seized his chest, leaving him weak and dizzy.

This must be love, he thought. *Like most human attributes, it is highly overrated.*

Smock dragged himself down the corridor to Wart's counseling office and rang the door chime. "What is it?" boomed Wart from within.

"May I see you, Counselor?" Smock called, gasping for breath. "I need a consultation on a private matter."

"Oh, all right," Wart grumbled.

As Smock entered, he saw that Wart was in the midst of a practice session with his Kringle battle axe. Wart slashed at the air, waving the axe in a ritualized sequence of motions. "What is the problem, Mr. Smock?" he asked without pausing.

"Would you like me to lie down on the couch as I describe my situation?" Smock inquired.

"Whatever," said Wart with a shrug. He continued to wave his weapon, parrying an imaginary opponent.

Smock stretched himself out on the patients' couch and began, "I am suffering from particularly acute bodily symptoms which I attribute to the emotion of love. I am obsessed with the thought of a certain woman, and she—" Smock broke off, disturbed that Wart's battle practice continued without even a glance in his direction. "Mr. Wart, shouldn't you be taking notes?"

Wart turned abruptly and held his axe high in the air, directly over Smock's head. "Do *not* tell a Kringle how to conduct his business!" Wart roared. Alarmed, Smock rose up on his elbows to a half-sitting position.

Wart raged, "It is bad enough that Starfreak ordered me into this job where I must listen to everyone talk about their *feelings*"—he spat out the word with distaste—"without some impudent patient telling me how to run my office!

"Now, I have a *system* here in the counseling center. You state your problem, and then I tell you how to get rid of it. Do you understand?"

"Yes, I do," Smock replied warily. Wart resumed his axe-swooping motions. Smock reclined again on the couch and folded his hands over his chest.

"As I was saying," Smock continued, "I am obsessed with the thought of a certain woman. She is so thoroughly human that I despair of becoming a worthy love match

"Mr. Wart, shouldn't you be taking notes?"

for her. Yet I cannot forget her. Day and night I dream about her, imagine her, sigh over her. In the grip of this deathless love, I pine for her. I wither like the reed in a parched land. My heart aches. My spirit grows weary. Tell me, Counselor Wart, what shall I do?"

Wart stopped swinging the axe long enough to scowl at Smock and deliver his treatment recommendation. "Snap out of it!" he growled.

Toward the end of that long, long day, Smock found himself consulting the professional of last resort: Chief Medical Officer Piker.

Smock's symptoms had grown so severe that he was barely conscious when he tottered into Sick Bay. Piker, sensing an interesting medical case in progress, waived the usual three-hour admittance routine and led Smock directly to the intensive care table.

Piker flattened Smock's tongue with a Popsicle stick and demanded, "Say 'aahhhh.' " Shining a flashlight at Smock's throat, Piker observed, "I see the problem right here. You have more than one uvula."

Piker straightened up importantly, adjusted the lapels of his white medical coat, and switched off the flashlight. "The 'uvula' is the term we medical people use for that fleshy thing that hangs above your tongue, way back in your throat," he said. "The word is right there in the medical dictionary, if you'd like to see for yourself. I found it this afternoon when I was looking up 'umbilical.' "

Smock nodded wearily. "I know what the uvula is, Mr. Piker," he rasped. "But *all* Vultures have more than one of them. Some Vultures have as many as four or five, though you only see those Vultures when the circus comes to town. No, I'm afraid the dual-uvula structure is not related to my symptoms."

"Hmmmmm," said Piker, gazing at him in an imitation of deep thought. Finally he asked, "What *are* your symptoms, anyway?"

Smock drew in a breath to answer, which triggered a coughing spasm deep in his chest. Piker grew alarmed watching Smock cough on and on and on, turning a deeper shade of red each time he hacked.

"Red Alert!" Piker declared. His medical staff snapped to attention, then stared at him, unsure what to do next. "No, that's not right," Piker checked himself. "Code Blue!"

At this command, several nurses wheeled a medical cart next to Smock's treatment table. One of them ripped open Smock's tunic and began prepping his chest for surgery. Another inserted an intravenous line into Smock's pointy eartip. A third went through his pockets looking for his insurance card.

Between gasps for breath, Smock managed to wheeze, "What . . . are you . . . going . . . to do?"

"Operate," Piker told him. "We'll have to remove some vital organs." A nurse helped Piker don his personalized surgical mask, which had strategically-placed cutouts in it to keep it from flattening his beard.

"But . . . " —Smock was beginning to black out— " . . . which ones?"

"Won't know till we get in there," Piker replied, his eyes glowing with the maniacal gleam of a surgeon on the hunt.

Later, back in Ten-Foreplay, Smock popped the top off a bottle of sparkling water, guzzled it down without pausing for breath, and reached for another. It was now three days since Piker had performed surgery on him, and this constant thirst seemed to be one of the side effects. Luckily, in his post as chief bartender, Smock had easy access to plenty of liquids during working hours.

To Smock's intense relief, Piker hadn't removed any vital organs after all. When Smock awoke in the recovery room, Piker had told him, "All I did was ream out your lungs." Piker had seemed disappointed that more invasive treatments had been impossible because his scalpel couldn't cut through Smock's tough Vulture innards.

One of them ripped open Smock's tunic.

Now, as Smock walked over to his bar sink to wash some glasses, once again he heard the strange *clank-clank* coming from his ribcage. This phenomenon, too, had arisen after his surgery.

Smock wondered if it was anything serious. It certainly interfered with his work behind the bar. If he didn't stand absolutely still while speaking to a customer or taking someone's drink order, the clanking noise drowned out their voices.

Smock told himself that this clanking was the reason he'd been putting off trying to contact Beverage Flusher again. He rationalized that it would be hard to conduct a sensitive conversation over this tumult, which sounded like a set of silverware churning around loose inside a dishwasher on the rinse cycle. But in his heart of hearts, Smock knew that he was simply afraid to approach Beverage again. She was probably still miffed that their last call had ended so abruptly, and Smock didn't know how to make amends for that.

How would a human male handle this situation? he wondered. *Perhaps a gift would be in order. What might she like?*

Unfamiliar with traditional offerings like candy or flowers, Smock tried to think of something that would appeal to Beverage's scientific interests. Finally he settled on a nice pair of skinfold calipers. As he agonized over whether to sign the gift tag "Yours, Mr. Smock" or "Affectionately, Mr. Smock," he saw Capt. Ricardo enter the door of Ten-Foreplay. Hurriedly Smock tucked the gift box under the counter.

"Captain," Smock said as Ricardo approached, "to what do we owe the pleasure of this unusual visit?"

To the surprise of Smock and everyone else nearby, Ricardo hoisted himself up and stood on a barstool. Reaching overhead with a screwdriver, he adjusted a small metal device attached to the ceiling tiles. Then he climbed down, dusted off the stool, sat on it, and motioned for Smock to lean in toward him. Smock did so, gingerly, trying not to clank.

Ricardo handed Smock a package. Inside it, Smock found several official-looking documents, some black and white 8″ x 10″ photographs, and an old-fashioned reel-to-reel audiotape.

Smock wound the tape onto a tape player he just happened to have behind the bar, adjusting the sound level so only he and Ricardo would be able to hear it. As he listened to the tape, he sifted through the documents.

"Good evening, Mr. Smock," said Ricardo's voice on the tape. "I have just disabled Starfreak's crew monitor in the ceiling because the confidential information you are about to hear requires the highest-level security clearance, and thus is not normally associated with your Starfreak-assigned position of chief bartender.

"As you know, we are supposed to find the Fountain of Youth, and our Bridge crew has been hard at work on this task. Please see photo number one." Photo number one showed the Bridge crew during the day shift. Guano sat in her position, reading *Mad* magazine; McCaw was at the Oops station, scowling; Ensign Roach manned the Conn, cleaning out her nose-bridge ridges with dental floss; and Ricardo sat in his command chair, commanding.

"Unfortunately," Ricardo's voice continued, "our atlas does not reveal the fountain's location, and another map which we often consult does not cover this sector. Please see document A." Smock lifted document A from the pile; it was a paper placemat from a fast-food restaurant, printed with a colorful children's treasure map.

There were other papers and photos; Smock hurriedly glanced through them as the reel of tape drew near its end.

"Your mission, should you decide to accept it," the audiotape said, "is to find out—from whatever source you can—exactly where this Fountain of Youth is located, and relay the coordinates to your captain before he leaves the bar this evening. As always, should you be captured and tortured, we will deny any knowledge of giving you this mission, and we will clean out your locker and sell its contents to pay storage costs. That is all. This tape will self-destruct in ten seconds."

Smock nodded to Ricardo, a movement which set off a series of clanks in Smock's chest.

As Smock headed for Ten-Foreplay's back room, the audiotape self-destructed via spontaneous combustion, sending up a cloud of greasy black smoke. This triggered a fire sprinkler in the ceiling, which doused Ricardo and several patrons sitting at the bar.

In the back room, Smock stepped into the walk-in cooler and powered up his shortwave radio.

Pondering what source to consult, Smock considered the fact that the Fountain of Youth's location was a deep dark secret. Not even his scientist pals, with whom he freely traded information, would know where it was.

He would have to consult the ultimate source of knowledge, the font of all wisdom, the keepers of even the most obscure yet vital facts in the universe. He dialed the frequency of the Milwaukee Public Library Ready Reference service and crossed his fingers.

Unfortunately, Smock had to lean forward awkwardly to use the radio; it rested on a stack of beer cases in the corner, which was the only available flat surface in the cooler. As he leaned, he couldn't help shifting around, and his interior clanking started up again.

"Hello. Ready Reference," said the consultant on the other end of the transmission.

"Hello," said Smock. "I wonder if you could tell me"—his innards went *clank-clank-clank*—"the location of" *clank-clank* "the Fountain of Youth."

"The Fountain of Truth?" repeated the consultant.

Clank-clank-clank. "What?" said Smock. "I'm sorry, I didn't—" *clank-clank-clankety-clank* "—hear you."

"Just a moment, sir . . ."—the consultant's words were

being drowned out on Smock's end—" ...I..." *clank* "-et that..." *clank-clank* "-formation..." *clank-clank-clank* " ...you."

As he waited on "hold," Smock worried whether he'd even be able to hear the information when it came. He turned the receiver up to full volume, and when the consultant came back on the line, her voice was loud enough to rattle the soda bottles next to the radio.

"THE COORDINATES ARE WEST 5555 BY SOUTH-WEST 90038," she told him.

"Thank you," Smock replied, his ears ringing. He clanked his way back to the bar. Ricardo, still dripping wet from his dousing by the fire sprinkler, glared at him.

"Sir, the coordinates are—" Smock began.

"I heard the coordinates, Mr. Smock," Ricardo snapped, "along with everyone else here in the lounge, and probably all the way to Deck Nineteen as well. This was supposed to be a secret mission, you know." Ricardo stood on the stool again and used his screwdriver to reactivate Starfreak's crew monitor in the ceiling.

Climbing off the stool, Ricardo left Smock with his parting shot: "You wouldn't need to do everything at top volume if you'd just turn down that horrid heavy metal music you've got on in here."

"Captain Smirk? This is LaForgery in Engineering." Georgie's voice came over the intercom of Smirk's ship, into the Ready Room where Smirk and Dacron were meeting. "Captain Ricardo's crew just made a drastic course alteration. They turned so abruptly that we lost all our momentum. We can catch them, but it looks like it'll take the remainder of our fuel. Is that what you want to do?"

"Yes, yes, do it!" Smirk replied impatiently. "Take care of it yourself, Mr. LaForgery. I've got an urgent matter to attend to here."

"Yes, sir." Georgie signed off the intercom.

Smirk leaned forward with his elbows on the desk and

said to Dacron, who sat in front of him, "The letter! Read the letter, Dacron." Then he held up his hand. "No, wait. Let me get in the mood to really enjoy this." He leaned back in the swivel chair with his arms behind his head, elbows out to the side. He closed his eyes, sighed deeply to focus his concentration, and said, "OK, now read it out loud to me."

Dacron held up the printout of the message from Deanna Troit which had arrived over his computer modem a few moments before. It was her first response to the love letters Dacron had sent her under Smirk's name.

"Dear Captain Smirk..." Dacron read. Smirk opened his eyes, looking disappointed.

"'Captain Smirk'?" he echoed. "I was hoping for at least 'Dear Jim.' 'Captain Smirk' is so formal."

"We did use 'Chief Engineer Troit' in the salutations I wrote, Captain," Dacron reminded him.

"Mmmm." Smirk nodded in agreement. "Well, next time let's move up to 'Dear Deanna.' All right, go on. I won't interrupt again."

Dacron read aloud:

Dear Captain Smirk,

It's impossible to remain angry with a man who composes such touching letters. Despite my resolve, I find myself writing this reply to you.

I was surprised to learn that you are within communication range of our ship, but then, down here in Engineering we don't really have a clue what's happening up on the Bridge. Rest assured that I will not tell Captain Ricardo you are so close; your presence shouldn't have any impact on our mission, whatever it is.

Your poetry skills have improved remarkably. More important, your letters show a thoughtful, sensitive, *human* side of your personality which you've never before revealed to me. Perhaps I was mistaken when I refused to give you another chance.

Let's continue this secret correspondence for now, until I can be sure that this change of heart is permanent and that you will not revert to being the chauvinistic jerk I used to know.

Sincerely,
Deanna Troit

"Wow!" Smirk exulted. "Is that great or what?!"

Dacron maintained his customary neutral expression, relieved that he didn't have to force a smile. It would have been hard to pretend happiness on Smirk's behalf when his own feelings were so jumbled.

On one hand, Dacron was delighted that his writing had been powerful enough to change Deanna's mind. On the other hand, he was envious that what she was changing her mind about was the possibility of resuming her romance with his boss.

Dacron wasn't sure where all this would lead. If his future letters were as persuasive as the previous ones had been, he might end up writing Deanna into Smirk's arms.

But Dacron didn't want to end the correspondence, even if Smirk hadn't been urging him on. He had to have some outlet for his newfound compulsion with Deanna. This ghostwriting scheme seemed the safest bet, for now. It let him express his genuine feelings for her without angering Smirk.

Jubilantly, Smirk swiveled back and forth in his chair. "Mr. LaForgery," he said to the intercom, "how long until we catch up to Ricardo's ship?"

"Captain," Georgie's voice answered, "the fuel supply is lower than I estimated. I've gone over the numbers several times, and we may not have enough power to reach them. And anyway, they're still taking the wrong course. We're actually closer to the Fountain of Youth where we are right now. Couldn't we just sit tight until they pass this way again?"

"No!" Smirk exclaimed. "It's urgent that we get back within communicator range of their ship. Do whatever you need to do to get us there, Mr. LaForgery."

Smirk swiveled to face Dacron. "Well, don't just sit there, Lieutenant," Smirk urged him. "Get going and start drafting my reply to Deanna. You've done a great job so far. Not bad for a guy with silicon chips where his heart should be."

Too
True

*S*TARDATE *44444.4 / 1350 hours*
   "This is Captain Smirk," said the recording. "I'm away from my command chair right now, so please leave a message at the tone. If you require immediate assistance, please press 'C' and ask the computer for help." *Beeeep.*

   "Captain, this is Georgie LaForgery in Engineering," Georgie said to the recorder. "We're really having problems down here. We've run out of Dilithium Crystal Vanish for the engines, just as I thought we would. Also, our sensors aren't working too well, and I don't know where we're going to get replacement parts, since only Starfreak carries them. We've also got to refill all the replicators with toner powder.

   "Oh, and one other thing—the subspace communicator is on the fritz, although that seems to be the least of our problems. I'll be working on repairs for these things, but it could take a while. LaForgery out."

1350½ hours
   "This is Chief Engineer Georgie LaForgery," said the recording. "I've stepped away from my work station for a moment to visit the men's room, but if you'd like to leave a message, I'll get back to you as soon as I can." *Beeeep.*

"I've stepped away from my work station to visit the men's room..."

"LaForgery, this is Captain Smirk," came Smirk's voice. "Forget all those other repairs for now and just concentrate on fixing the subspace communicator. It's vital that we get it working again."

1430 hours
"This is Captain Smirk," said the recording. "I've gone to the gym to play racquetball, so please leave a message at the tone." *Beeeep.*

"Captain, this is your first officer, Dacron," said the android. "Mr. LaForgery and I have been working on the subspace communicator, as you requested. It will take several days, at least, to restore its ability to send messages. However, we *have* enabled it to *receive* messages. If any letters should arrive from Deanna Troit, I will forward them to you immediately. Dacron out."

A series of love notes began piling up on Capt. Smirk's desk. Each night he sifted through the pile, growing increasingly frustrated as he wondered how long it would be before Dacron could answer them for him.

Stardate 44445.4

Dear Jim,
   It's been a while since I've heard from you, and I wonder how you're doing. I miss the poetry you've been sending. Please write soon.

Sincerely,
Deanna

Stardate 44446.4

Dear Jim,
   Your sudden silence intrigues me. Are you busy with some new adventure? I've re-read all your let-

I'm eager for more. When will you

Fondly,
Deanna

Stardate 44449.1

Dear Jim,

I'm dying to read more of your tender poetry. I know you must be busy, but can't you write something? Not even a limerick to tide me over?

This ship, and in particular my assigned post in Engineering, is the most unromantic place imaginable. A love note from you would be a welcome relief.

Achingly,
Deanna

Like Capt. Smirk, Dr. Beverage Flusher also began accumulating a stack of correspondence. In her case, the letters came from Mr. Smock. She read and re-read his messages, growing certain that his affection would flicker out before the Have-Nots' communicator would be repaired and she could answer him.

Stardate 44446.7

Dear Dr. Flusher:

Please forgive the abrupt conclusion to our recent telephone conversation. A health emergency intervened before I could say goodbye. In fact, it is for health reasons that I resort to writing to you rather than calling again. My physical condition makes it difficult to carry on a normal conversation.

I trust you are well and having success in your

medical career. Would it be too bold of me to ask if your invitation to dinner is still open?

Sincerely yours,
Mr. Smock

Stardate 44448.2

Dear Dr. Flusher:

Since I have not had the pleasure of a reply from you as yet, I trust that you need more time to consider whether or not to dine with me. Please take as long as you need to decide.

In the meantime, here is a copy of a particularly fascinating article from the *Journal of Brownian Motion*. I hope you think of me as you read it.

Sincerely yours,
Mr. Smock

Stardate 44449.4

Dear Dr. Flusher:

Please forgive me for raising the issue of us having dinner together. It must have angered you, for you have not replied to my letters. I deeply regret my impudence. It will not happen again.

I will take your refusal to reply as a signal that you are no longer interested in pursuing a social relationship with me. And though this will be the last of my letters, I shall always hold your image in my mind with the highest regard.

Sincerely yours,
Mr. Smock

After sending off his final message to Dr. Flusher, Smock forced himself to get back to work. The Haves' ship had just arrived at another planet, and Ricardo ordered Smock to join the Away Team traveling down to its surface.

Moments later, the Away Team of Smock, Guano and Troit stood on the UltraFax platform, waiting to beam down to the coordinates Smock had been given by Ready Reference—not realizing that their crew had inadvertently sought out the Fountain of Truth.

"I hope you made sure to lay in the right beam-down coordinates this time, Checkout," Guano griped. "I don't want to end up in the ladies' room, standing in the bidet."

Checkout scowled at her. "Dey are correct," he snapped, energizing the UltraFax beam.

Indeed, the coordinates were right on target. In fact, Checkout was a little too accurate. He beamed the trio right into the middle of the fountain, where a continuous plume of water cascaded high into the air and splashed back down into the pool, churning its surface.

The sudden drenching in the Fountain of Truth drew shrieks from Guano and Troit. They headed for the side, but the slick bottom of the pool made movement difficult, and both of them slipped and plunged backwards. Smock, meanwhile, was slaking his intense thirst with big gulps of the fountain's water.

Troit took another step toward the edge, slipped again, and fell back with a splash. The impact tore loose an underwire from her bra, leaving her looking rather lopsided. The wire bounced away in the dancing waters.

Troit shook her dripping hair out of her eyes. "Mr. Smock!" she called out. "Here we are practically drowning, and you're standing there taking a drink. Get your Vulture butt over here and help us!"

"Cool your jets, Counselor," Smock replied. "I am thirsty. You can either wait till I have finished drinking or find your own way out of this fountain."

Guano eyed them curiously. She'd already realized that this wasn't the Fountain of Youth, since none of them were looking any younger. *But what fountain is it?* she wondered. *What would make these two speak their minds for a change? They both usually behave like diplomats.*

Guano dog-paddled her way to the fountain's edge and scrambled over the side. A few paces away, she found a sign:

**Fountain of Truth
Caution: ingestion may be fatal to politicians**

Guano wasn't sure whether this water would prove valuable, but rather than waste any time wondering about it, she immediately began gathering the water into jugs and stashing them in her hat. She had a good supply by the time Troit and Smock finally emerged from the fountain. They contacted the ship, told Capt. Ricardo that this wasn't the right place, either, and Faxed back up. The ship left the orbit of the planet, and the Haves resumed their search.

Stardate 44449.7 / 0950 hours

Dear Capt. Smirk:
   All right, buster, why haven't you answered my letters? I'm tired of being nice about this! I've been pretending it doesn't bother me, but it does.
   I must have been crazy to think that you had actually changed your ways. Apparently you're still the inconsiderate creep I remember so well from our engagement, because as soon as I respond to your moves, you flake out on me again. Well, let me tell you, unless I hear from you SOON, we're finished!
                                                Assertively,
                                                Deanna Troit

Stardate 44449.7 / 0951 hours
   "This is First Officer Dacron," said the recording. "At the moment I am plugged into the wall outlet to recharge my batteries, so I cannot speak to you in person. However, if you leave a message at the tone, I will answer it promptly and in exhaustive detail." *Beeeep.*

"If you leave a message at the tone, I will answer it promptly and in exhaustive detail."

"Dacron!" came Smirk's holler into the recorder. "How can you rest at a time like this? We've got to get that subspace communicator working again so we can answer Deanna's letters! We—oh, never mind—I'll come over there myself to get you in gear..."

"I am sorry, sir, but I cannot possibly drink another drop." Dacron stared dazedly at the empty cans of Mountain Dew littering the floor around him. "In fact," he added, "I find it difficult to believe that my body has already retained this much liquid."

"Just try to drink a little more," Capt. Smirk urged him, hovering over the chair in which Dacron sat in a corner of Engineering. "He's got room for more, hasn't he, Georgie? You're our resident android expert."

Georgie shook his head and said, "I think he's just about reached his limit, Captain."

"But he doesn't seem any more alert than when we started," Smirk observed. "You said this stuff is even better than coffee at making him hyper."

"It'll just be a little longer. Then the caffeine will kick in," Georgie reassured Smirk. "That should recharge him in a big way. It'll be the equivalent of spending ten hours plugged into the wall outlet."

"I hope you're right," Smirk replied. "He's got to work at top speed to fix the subspace communicator. Not to mention all the other things that are broken around here." Smirk glanced impatiently at his watch. "How much longer?"

"Ten seconds more," said Georgie, consulting his own watch. "Five, four, three, two, one...now."

A spasm seized Dacron's body, and his head snapped to attention. He leaped out of the chair. "INTRIGUING!" he shouted. "My heart rate just accelerated two hundred and fifteen percent!"

"Let's get him over to the communicator," Georgie directed. He and Smirk steered Dacron to a panel at the wall; it opened to reveal the inner workings of the subspace communicator's main junction box. Dacron worked furiously at the panel, his hands moving so fast that they blurred. A few seconds later he reported, "Sending mode of subspace communicator has been restored." He looked around with nervous, birdlike movements. "What shall I work on next?"

As Georgie led Dacron to another task, Smirk eagerly opened a channel on the subspace communicator so they could contact Troit on Ricardo's ship. However, the signal still wasn't getting through; the monitors indicated that Ricardo's ship had moved out of range into another LATA zone. Frustrated, Smirk switched off the set.

"LaForgery!" Smirk said. "Get Dacron working on the engines next. We've got to get closer to Ricardo's ship."

"Aye, sir," Georgie said.

A few minutes later, Smirk's crew was underway with the engines humming at Warped 9, thanks to Dacron's speedy invention of a Dilithium Crystal Vanish substitute.

During the next few hours, Dacron took advantage of his nervous energy. He refilled the replicators, performed a full diagnostic of the ship's built-in vaccum cleaning ducts, mopped the Mess Hall floors, and discovered a cure for cancer. He was working on the faulty sensors when Smirk paged him from the Bridge.

"Dacron," Smirk said, "we've arrived at a planet. Our sensors indicate that this was the latest stop that Ricardo's crew made. I want you and Beverage to Fax down there and see what's happening."

"Should I finish repairing the sensors first, Captain?" Dacron asked. "We cannot be sure they are reliable."

"No," Smirk replied. "I want to stay hot on Ricardo's trail. We know his ship has been here recently, and they're probably still in orbit. They might have somebody down on the surface. Check it out."

"Yes, sir," Dacron said.

Luckily, Ricardo's Away Team had left a lot of stray

UltraFax particles lying around, thanks to Checkout's sloppy beam-down technique; so Smirk's UltraFax chief, O'Brine, had no trouble tracing the exact spot of their landing. Noticing that there was a body of water at that spot, O'Brine shifted his UltraFax beam several meters to the left.

Dacron and Beverage materialized a few steps away from the Fountain of Truth. Beverage walked over to investigate the sign identifying the fountain. As Dacron scanned the area for any indication of Ricardo's crew, he noticed the sunlight gleaming off an object that bounced in the fountain's churning water.

Searching his memory banks, Dacron instantly identified the object as the underwire of a woman's bra, and his lover's intuition told him it belonged to Deanna Troit. Dacron's pulse, already soaring from the Mountain Dew, raced even faster. Impulsively he jumped into the fountain to retrieve the underwire.

"Dacron! What are you doing?" Beverage called. Dacron waded back toward the edge, triumphantly holding the wire high in the air. Beverage helped him step out of the fountain.

"I could not resist retrieving this precious possession of Deanna Troit," Dacron said. "It is a remnant of her delicate lingerie. She must have left it here accidentally. I will cherish it forever."

"What in the world—?" Beverage shook her head in confusion. "Dacron, what are you saying?"

"This is a keepsake from the object of my passion," Dacron explained. "I am deeply, madly, achingly in love with Deanna Troit."

"But you can't feel love—" Beverage began. Then realization dawned in her eyes. "That fall into the Fountain of Love is still affecting you . . . " she said slowly as she figured it out, " . . . and now this Fountain of Truth . . . so you can't keep it to yourself . . . "

"This is too wonderful to keep to myself!" Dacron cried.

He jumped up onto the flat edge of the low wall encircling the fountain and lifted his arms toward the sky. "I want the universe to know that I love Deanna," he proclaimed. "And furthermore, she loves me."

Dacron began dancing back and forth along the wall. "She does not know it yet, because she thinks all those love letters came from Captain Smirk. But it was my writing that won her heart!"

Bev's eyes widened. "You've been writing love letters to Deanna and putting the captain's name on them?" she asked.

"Yes! He asked me to ghostwrite for him. But the words were all mine," Dacron exulted, hopping up and down, "and they were sincere. And I must tell her so!"

"Dacron, are you crazy?" Beverage pulled him off the wall and grasped his shoulders, trying to hold him still. "Stop dancing for a minute and listen to me," she ordered, looking him straight in the eye. With an effort, Dacron tamed down his jumping motion to a nervous jiggle.

"You can't just go blurting out all this," Beverage told him. "Captain Smirk will be furious if you blow his cover. You know how much he's counting on getting back together with Deanna."

Anxiety clouded Dacron's expression. "That is true," he said. "Everything we have done on this mission has been directed to that end." He looked even more worried as he added, "But I must tell everyone the truth. I cannot seem to keep it to myself."

"You're going to have to," Beverage said. "Do you want the captain to shut you down? He'll do that, you know. He'll open your back panel, press your 'off' switch and throw away the key. Unless..." Bev got a thoughtful gleam in her eye.

"Unless what, Doctor?" Dacron asked anxiously. "Please help me. I have no skill for office politics."

"Unless I shut you down, and bring you back up whenever he's not around," Bev went on, making up a scheme as she went along. "We could keep you in Sick Bay; I'll say you've been damaged by falling into the fountain. When you're awake, we'll restrain you somehow so you can't blurt out anything over the communication channels . . . he'll surely be monitoring them. Then, when we finally catch up with the other ship, you can go see Deanna in person and tell her the truth."

A yellow tear formed in the corner of Dacron's eye. "You would do all that for me?" he asked, choked with emotion. "That is so kind of you, Doctor."

Beverage smiled and gave a little shrug. "I'd like to see true love win out for a change," she confessed. For a moment, her thoughts drifted back over her own unlucky love life.

Her husband, Jock Flusher, had been killed in action many years ago. Poignantly enough, Capt. Ricardo himself had delivered Jock's body to Beverage; that was back when Ricardo was still moonlighting for UPS.

Much later, she'd fallen for an alien being, only to discover that his handsome outer body was merely a host for his true inner entity, which looked like a cow's stomach. When the host body died, Dr. Flusher had transplanted this throbbing mass into a series of temporary hosts: first Cmdr. Piker, then an alien woman, and finally a laboratory chimpanzee.

Despite all this turmoil, she'd still planned to marry the cow's-stomach essence of her lover, but Starfreak refused to honor their application for a marriage license because they'd filled in the blank for "groom's species" with the notation "subject to change." The affair had ended on a bittersweet note, and Flusher still felt uneasy whenever the Mess Hall menu featured tripe.

And now, Flusher realized sadly, her inability to answer Smock's letters had ruined their budding relationship before it even got off the ground. She began thinking out loud: "In fact, I thought even I had a shot at love, but it seems to have died on the vine. . . . "

Capt. Ricardo himself had delivered Jock's body to
Beverage.

She waved her hand, dismissing the thought. "Never mind," she said to Dacron. "We've got to get you to Sick Bay and pretend you've been damaged. Let's hope this works."

Truth's
Consequences

"**C**OME WITH ME , Deanna. Please?" Guano pleaded, tagging along as Deanna Troit performed routine maintenance of the engines of Ricardo's ship. "I really want to get to the bottom of this thing about your mother and the computer," said Guano. "Ever since we fell into that Fountain of Truth, it's been bugging me."

"I know. You've hardly stopped talking about it since the minute we got back," said Troit, flushing some Dilithium Crystal Vanish into the engine's Main Bowl.

Troit admitted, "You've even got *me* interested in finding out the truth about the computer. I guess I'll go with you. But this won't be easy. You know we're going to have to talk directly to the CPU—the Central Processing Unit."

Guano nodded. "I know. I just didn't want to go alone." They headed down the corridor toward the Crewmover.

"You really think my mother's involved with the computer in some way?" Troit asked.

"You heard what everybody said when we asked around in Ten-Foreplay this morning—how they think of her whenever the computer speaks, and how nobody has ever talked to them both at the same time," said Guano. "The whole thing is pretty fishy. Now if you ask the computer something that only your mother would know, maybe we can trick it into revealing the connection. Maybe the computer is tied into her modem or something."

"I'll try," said Troit, "but have you ever met the CPU in person?" Guano shook her head. "It's awfully intimidating," Troit continued. "That's why most of the crew only hears the audio. It's pretty hard to deal with the CPU face-to-face."

They rode the Crewmover to Lower Level 68 in the depths of the *Endocrine's* basement. The door opened onto a cavernous, dimly-lit room, and a damp, musty odor hit their nostrils.

Programmer gnomes scurried about, adjusting the tubing and wiring that snaked out to all areas of the ship. At the far end of the room sat the CPU, flashing its lights and pouring smoke from its exhaust valves. In front of it, a hologram of a huge turbaned female head floated in midair, shrouded in fog.

Terrified, Guano froze in her tracks. Troit clutched Guano's hand and pulled her forward.

"Who dares to approach the CPU?" thundered the hologram head. The programmers squeaked, scuttling out of the way.

Troit raised her chin and quavered, "Deanna Troit." She curtsied.

"Deanna Troit, eh? Well, you'd better have a good reason for bothering me, Troit, 'cause I know where you hang out, and I might just decide to zap you someday," sneered the computer's hologram head. Then it glared at Guano, demanding, "And who are you?"

Guano bit her nails and tried to hide behind Troit, who pushed her out front again.

"Me?" Guano squealed. "I'm uh, um . . . Rita Miller."

"We have come to ask you a question, Your Magnificence," Troit began.

"Why can't you use the audio channel like you're supposed to?" the computer scolded.

"It's sort of a delicate topic," said Troit. "We didn't think

"Who dares to approach the CPU?"

you'd want to talk about it in front of everybody."

"Hmmmph," the computer sniffed. "All right, let's hear it."

"Well, as you know, Christmas is coming," Troit said, "and I'd like to buy my mother a present, and as you probably also know, she prefers low-cut gowns, which she buys at Frederick's of Hubble ... "

"Will you get to the point?" the computer raged, with a flash of its strobe lights and a puff of smoke for emphasis.

"So I was wondering"—Troit's words rushed out—"whether you've got some sort of inventory of her wardrobe so I don't buy her something she already has."

"How should I know what clothing your mother owns?" bellowed the computer. Volcanic sound effects boomed out of its speakers, shaking the walls. Troit and Guano reflexively took a step backward. "Am I your mother's keeper? What a question to ask of Starfreak's most advanced processing unit!"

"Well, you've answered more trivial questions than that," said Troit. "Last week I heard you and Ensign Roach talking about the world record in the ninety-and-over age division of the women's triple jump—"

"SILENCE!" thundered the computer. "I will not deign to consider your request. Now get out of here, you miserable blobs of organic matter!"

"But—" Troit protested.

"GET OUT! BEAT IT! AMSCRAY! The Great and Powerful Computer has spoken!" To emphasize its point, the CPU threw out a bolt of electricity, knocking Troit to her knees.

"Hey!" yelled Guano. "Why'd you do that? You big bully!" She helped Troit to her feet. "You didn't even answer our question, you big blustering wall of microchips!"

The CPU's hologram face narrowed its eyes and sneered, "Button your lip, you ... you ... creature with no eyebrows, you."

"Oh yeah? Who's gonna make me?" Guano challenged, rolling up her sleeves.

"I know what you're thinking," the CPU hissed. "You think I've got something to hide. You think you're going to discover the truth about my identity."

"Huh?" said Guano.

"What do you mean? How can you know what she's thinking?" asked Troit.

"Nothing," the computer replied quickly. "Nothing. Just forget it."

But their suspicions had been intensified, and now Guano noticed a curtain fluttering at the side of the CPU. She motioned to Troit. Silently they approached the curtain as the computer continued blustering and throwing off smoke.

Guano drew aside the curtain. Troit gasped: "Mother!"

There behind the curtain, working an assortment of levers and buttons on a control panel, was Woksauna Troit. She gave them a startled glance, then leaned toward her microphone. "Pay no attention to that woman behind the curtain!" she said. Her voice boomed from the CPU speakers. "The Great and Powerful Computer . . . uh . . . "

Seeing that Guano and Troit weren't falling for it, Woksauna stopped the charade and primly smoothed back her hair. "Hello, spittle one," she said, greeting her daughter with a pet name from childhood. "Hello, *Guano*," she added with a mean look.

"Mother, how could you?" Deanna said with a sigh. "You, of the Betavoid royal House of Pancakes, keeper of the sacred griddle—moonlighting as a computer?"

Woksauna looked embarrassed, but she defended herself stoutly. "What else am I to do? There are only so many key staff positions for a women of my . . . of a certain age. Besides, this job lets me keep an eye on you, Deanna. The computer has video cameras trained on every area of the ship.

"Which reminds me," she continued, wagging an index finger at her daughter, "I see you've been playing around with that Piker fellow again. How many times must I tell you? A man never buys the cow when he can get the milk for free."

While Guano and Troit were confronting the computer in the basement, Mr. Smock stomped down the hall toward Sick Bay, determined to find out what was wrong with him.

He had to get rid of these horrible post-surgical symptoms. As long as he kept clanking and rattling and running off to get a drink of water every few minutes, he couldn't hope to approach Beverage Flusher if their paths should ever cross again. He was counting on his next Away Team mission to provide that opportunity.

After falling into the Fountain of Truth, Smock had made up his mind to tell Dr. Flusher how he really felt about her. He figured he had nothing to lose by trying the direct approach, since his highly circumspect letters to her had gone unanswered. An old saying of Capt. Smirk's popped into his head: "When all else fails, tell the truth."

But first Smock had to conquer these nagging physical problems, and he no longer had any qualms about pinpointing their source: Chief Medical Officer Wilson Piker.

Smock burst through the entrance of Sick Bay. "Sir, do you have an appointment?" asked the receptionist, rising to intercept him; but he strode past her into the examination area.

Piker was on duty, studying a patient's severely fractured leg and tapping a reflex hammer around the wound. "Tell me where it hurts," he ordered.

"Aaaaaagh!" the patient screamed as Piker struck the wound directly.

Piker looked surprised at this violent reaction, but before he could raise his hammer to make another diagnostic test, Smock grabbed him by the lapels of his medical jacket and shoved him against the wall. "What the—" Piker stammered.

"Listen, you quack," Smock snarled. "I've been feeling

terrible ever since you performed surgery on me. I don't expect you to be able to figure out your own mistakes, but perhaps, in spite of you, I can find out just what went wrong during that operation." With that, Smock pressed his thumb along Piker's jawbone and his fingers against Piker's temple and cheekbone, engaging Piker in the famous Vulture mind-melt.

Smock realized that in this case it might be hard to tell when the mind-melt took effect. Usually the meltee's suddenly-vacant expression was the definitive sign, but Piker always looked pretty vacant anyway. However, when Smock's mind filled with a serious of vacuous images a moment later, he knew he'd gotten in.

The theme music from "Petticoat Junction" was playing over and over in Piker's brain. Smock pressed past that and drove deeper, into the memory region.

It was cluttered with trivia. Smock searched through clusters of Piker's favorite lottery numbers, Kringle recipes and jazz trombone solos until finally he found Piker's memory of the surgery. It was frustratingly vague, but Smock did get the impression that somehow Piker had messed up the protocol toward the end of the procedure.

Disappointed, Smock backed out of Piker's brain and ended the mind-melt. He drew his fingers away from Piker's face.

Piker moaned. "My brain hurts," he complained. "This is like being back in school."

Smock left Sick Bay but returned just a few minutes later accompanied by Dr. McCaw, who climbed onto the surgery table so he could reach the crew monitor Starfreak had placed on the ceiling.

"Hey, what do you think you're doing?" Piker demanded. "That table is supposed to be sterile, you know—so we can play poker on it while we eat lunch."

"Well, then, wipe it off after I'm done with it," McCaw retorted, climbing back down to the floor. "Haven't you ever heard of Lysol?"

Smock drove deeper into Piker's memory.

"And how come you're here, anyway?" Piker went on. "You belong on the Bridge. I'm the chief medical officer now."

"Not for the next couple of hours, you're not," said McCaw. "Jean-Lucy agreed that I could come in here and perform surgery on Mr. Smock, to figure out where you screwed up."

"Has Starfreak authorized your change of duties?" Piker wanted to know.

"Of course they haven't, you nincompoop!" McCaw barked. "Why do you think I disabled the ceiling monitor? If we waited for all the paperwork involved in a Starfreak authorization, Mr. Smock could die of thirst. Or noise pollution. Or whatever other symptoms he's got, thanks to your incompetence."

McCaw motioned for Smock to lie on the table and began prepping him for surgery. McCaw explained to Piker, "Ricardo said to go ahead with this make-good operation. We'll get the authorization later by pretending we haven't yet performed the surgery, so eventually the HMO will reimburse us. I've done it this way millions of times."

"Hmmmph," Piker grunted.

"I'll need an assistant," McCaw said, donning a blue gown and mask. "Who's your best surgical nurse?"

Piker frowned and admitted grumpily, "Miss Ames, I guess."

"Well, get her over here," McCaw ordered. A moment later, the nurse appeared at his side. McCaw glanced at her, then did a double take and inquired, "What happened to your arm?"

"It's artificial, sir," Nurse Ames replied.

"I can see that," McCaw snapped, "but it seems so awkward—here, let me have a look." He grasped the limb, gave it a cursory glance, and asked her, "Who installed this thing?"

"Chief Medical Officer Piker, of course," she said.

"Well, he put it on backwards," McCaw said. "After I've

finished using the table, ask him to fix it for you. Right now, get me someone else to help with this surgery. I don't want a backhanded assistant."

Nurse Ames disappeared, and soon another nurse stepped up to McCaw's side. "Nurse Hatchet at your service, Dr. McCaw," she reported.

"Hatchet, set up the anesthesia," McCaw said. She nodded and went to the corner to retrieve a large rubber mallet. "What's that?" McCaw asked.

"It's Mr. Piker's way of putting patients under," Nurse Hatchet told him. "He says it's quicker and easier than gas."

McCaw gave her his distinctive look of disdain, perfected through years of practice; it managed to convey his displeasure even though most of his face was covered by the surgical mask and cap. "I can see this is going to be a long day," he groused.

Two hours later, Dr. McCaw finally finished the surgery on Mr. Smock. A metal pan at McCaw's elbow held the objects he'd retrieved from Smock's innards—things that Piker had inadvertently left behind during the previous surgery: five surgical instruments, a pair of latex gloves, a dozen sponges, and several insurance reimbursement forms.

Back on the Bridge, Capt. Ricardo waited anxiously for the surgery to be finished. The sooner Smock recovered, the sooner he'd be able to re-query his secret source of information about the location of the Fountain of Youth.

The Haves' Bridge crew desperately needed Smock's help. On their own, they still hadn't gotten any closer to discovering where the fountain might be. The best they had come up with was to notice a bunch of youthful-looking aliens traveling out of the LaLa Quadrant. They had projected back to the source of the travelers, only to discover that it was a starbase specializing in plastic surgery.

Ricardo wondered gloomily whether the Romanumens might actually beat them to the Fountain of Youth, and if so, whether Admiral Nonsequitur would follow through on his threat to lay off all of them. *Maybe I could take an early retirement instead,* Ricardo speculated. *Or better yet, go back to serve on my former ship, the USS* Skinbracer.

Several days later, on Capt. Smirk's ship, Dacron sat twiddling his thumbs in the research lab of Sick Bay. Beverage Flusher provided him this sanctuary so Capt. Smirk wouldn't realize he was fully operational and liable at any moment to blurt out the truth, the whole truth, and nothing but the truth.

After Bev and Dacron had beamed back to Sick Bay from the Fountain of Truth, Bev had turned him off and laid him on an examining table. Smirk came in for a progress report, saw Dacron sprawled out on the table, and bought Bev's story that Dacron was damaged during the away mission. After Smirk left Sick Bay, Bev turned Dacron back on.

Smirk hadn't returned since then; and because the research lab was tucked deep within Sick Bay, they felt sure that he couldn't unexpectedly walk in on Dacron without being intercepted by Bev.

Dacron was locked in this inner room. "It's for your own protection," Bev reminded him. "You won't have a chance to tell anybody about your crush on Deanna."

Dacron passed the time by monitoring a special long-range sensor array he'd rigged up. Bev had made sure that the equipment could not send audio or visual messages, which might be monitored by the captain. All Dacron could do was listen to the sensor speakers, hour after hour, but it was better than doing nothing.

There had been no more messages from Ricardo's ship; Deanna Troit had stopped writing, just as she'd threatened to do. Dacron wondered if he would ever get the chance to explain everything to her in person.

Amidst the sensors' humming and hissing with routine transmissions and static, one signal suddenly caught Dacron's attention. As he listened more closely, he realized this was indeed an important development. He had tapped into the radio of the Romanumen flagship *Brassiere*.

Dacron knew that no one else on the ship would have caught this transmission, and the information was vital. He had to tell Capt. Smirk.

"What is it, Dacron?" Beverage asked a few moments later. "The nurse said you insisted on seeing me immediately."

"Doctor, I must speak to the captain," Dacron declared. "The Romanumens are about to arrive at the Fountain of Youth. If they claim the fountain, Starfreak will have no chance of recovering it. I can help us get there first, if I am able to work at my Oops station.

"You said my condition of excessive truthfulness will last indefinitely," Dacron continued, "but can you give me something to temporarily suppress it so I may serve on the Bridge until we have completed our mission?"

"Gee, Dacron, that's a tough one," Bev said, thinking hard.

"Is there some medicine that might work?" Dacron asked. "It need only last for a few hours."

"There *is* an old folk remedy...." Bev said to herself. "I wonder if I still have some of that around...." She headed for the medicine closet with Dacron trailing her eagerly. After rummaging through the clutter in the back of the closet, Bev pulled out a bottle. "Aha!" she said. "Here it is."

She blew the dust off the label, which read "Essence of Bureaucracy."

"This suppresses the ability to give straight answers," Bev said. "I'm not sure what dosage to give you, though," she continued, reading the fine print on the label. "Too much, and you'll go into a stupor; too little, and you'll still be blurting out the truth about Deanna. Well, let's

start with a tablespoonful, and I'll monitor you as you talk
to Captain Smirk."

Beep-beep boop-boop went the door chime of Capt. Smirk's
Ready Room. Smirk stood by the side wall, fooling around
with the model of the *Endocrine* that sat on a pedestal.
He pushed the model back and forth while making Warped
engine noises: *vrooom, vrooom.* "Come in," he called toward the door.

Dacron and Bev entered. "Ah, Dacron," said Smirk.
"Good to see you up and about again."

"Thank you, sir," Dacron began. He glanced nervously
at Beverage, then went on, "Captain, I have intercepted
an important message from the Romanumen flagship."

Smirk pushed aside the model *Endocrine* and turned
his attention to Dacron. "Yes?"

"They now know the exact location of the Fountain of
Youth, and they are headed there at top speed," Dacron
told him. "I have calculated a method by which our ship
might exceed its normal engine capacity so we could arrive
before they do. It would involve constant, subtle modifi-
cations of the ship's engines. I believe I can best direct
this effort from my station on the Bridge."

Smirk was all business. "Well, let's get going!" He
started toward the door but stopped when Dacron spoke
up again.

"I must emphasize, Captain," Dacron continued, "that
there is no margin for error. Your previous plan to hold
back and then dash in for a dramatic rescue at the last
minute would jeopardize this mission."

"I understand, Dacron," Smirk said. "We'll concentrate
on getting to the fountain before the Romanumens do.
And at least we'll beat Ricardo there, which should con-
vince Starfreak to reinstate our crew to full-time status."
He headed for the door, then stopped again as Dacron
resumed his spiel.

"It would be a grievous error to play coy, merely for

dramatic effect," said Dacron, "and lose the chance to claim the fountain for Starfreak just so you could impress Dea—"

Abruptly Beverage jerked Dacron by the arm. "Dacron!" she interrupted, pulling him toward the far corner. She smiled at Smirk and said, "Excuse us for a moment, Captain." Spinning Dacron around to face her, she forced his mouth open and poured several gulps of Essence of Bureaucracy down his throat, straight from the bottle.

Dacron swallowed hard, blinking his eyes. "Thank you, Doctor," he said. "That is much better."

"What was that you were saying, Dacron?" Capt. Smirk prompted.

"Nothing of importance, sir," Dacron replied. "It would be best for us to proceed with our mission immediately."

Beverage sighed with relief and followed Dacron and Smirk as they headed for their stations on the Bridge.

Dacron gave their pilot the precise coordinates of the Fountain of Youth in the Hydrant Quadrant, and she laid in the course. As the ship sped toward their destination, Dacron used the intercom to stay in contact with Georgie in Engineering, suggesting a series of adjustments to the engines for maximum output.

Beverage sat in the command chair to Smirk's left. She tried not to be too obvious about watching Dacron for any telltale signs of hyperhonesty. So far, he was holding up all right.

After they had traveled for about an hour, Westerly noticed a signal on the radar at his Tactical station. "Captain Smirk," he reported, "our course is taking us close to Captain Ricardo's ship."

"Really?" Smirk straightened up in his chair. He told the pilot, "Slow to Warped 3.14 so we can check this out," and then asked Westerly, "What are they doing?"

"Not much, sir," Westerly observed. "They're orbiting an American Automobile Association tourist information center."

"Probably asking for directions," Smirk said with a chuckle. "Let's listen in on their communication transmissions, just for kicks. Monitor the audio channel from their ship, Mr. Flusher. Put it over our Bridge speakers."

"Aye, sir." Westerly pressed the control buttons. Unfortunately, being away at Starfreak Academy Film School had left Westerly's skills a little rusty, and he inadvertently put the radio into its default mode that allowed two-way communication. Unknown to him and the rest of Smirk's Bridge crew, anything they said would now be heard on Ricardo's Bridge.

A few moments later, they heard Mr. Snot tell Capt. Ricardo, "Cap'n, we've got a message comin' in from Starfreak Headquarters."

"Onscreen," came Ricardo's voice.

Smirk cocked his eyebrow in a this-ought-to-be-interesting expression and tipped his head, the better to hear the broadcast of Ricardo's conversation.

"Captain Ricardo," came the voice of Admiral Nonsequitur.

"Admiral," replied Ricardo, sounding a little nervous. "We've been meaning to call you. We'd like special dispensation for Dr. McCaw to perform surgery on Mr. Smock. You see—"

"Never mind, Ricardo," Nonsequitur interrupted. "We have something far more important to deal with. Starfreak has just intercepted a coded Romanumen message sent by the wartbird *Brassiere* to the Romanumen headquarters. The ship reported that they're zeroing in on the Fountain of Youth. Do you know what this means?"

"I suppose, Admiral," Ricardo said in an abject tone, "it means that they're about to beat us to the punch."

"They are?" Nonsequitur seemed amazed. "Yes, yes, Ricardo. You're right! Of all the rotten—they're going to beat us to the punch!"

Smirk shook his head gleefully, knowing his crew would forestall this disaster. He beamed at Beverage, and she smiled back, sharing his delight.

They heard Ricardo suggest weakly, "We could follow their ship and try to cut them off at the last minute..."

"That won't work," Nonsequitur said. "You'll never find them. They've got that device turned on, that thing that makes their ship invisible—what is it called? Choking device? Joking device?"

Ricardo supplied the term. "Croaking device."

"Yes, the croaking device," said Nonsequitur. "So the only way we could hope to beat them there would be to start now and outrace them. But we can't do that without knowing the exact location of the fountain. If only we knew where it is..."

Sitting at his Oops station, Dacron began panting as the Essence of Bureaucracy wore off. Powerful pro-honesty forces sought to loosen his tongue: years of Starfreak training to supply information whenever a superior officer needed it... the Fountain of Truth water that had saturated his synthetic pores... and the aftereffects of the Mountain Dew, which still kept his system in overdrive. Even the knowledge that he would cook his own goose by blurting out the truth was no match for the compulsion to blab.

"The Fountain of Youth is in the Hydrant Quadrant," Dacron said aloud. "The precise coordinates are North 2389 by Northwest 6751."

"Who said that?" came Nonsequitur's voice over the intercom.

This was immediately followed by Ricardo's voice, which echoed, "North 2389 by Northwest 6751?"

A look of horror spread across Smirk's face. "They can hear us!" he gasped.

"Smirk, is that you?" Nonsequitur's voice inquired.

As realization dawned, Smirk involuntarily followed the path of error around his Bridge. He glared at Dacron, swiveled backward to shoot a dirty look at Westerly Flusher, then snapped his gaze up toward the ceiling where the communicator's microphone hung.

"They can hear us! Good grief!" Smirk shrieked. Everyone on his Bridge froze in disbelief for a moment as they realized what had just happened.

Then they heard Capt. Ricardo order, "Ensign Roach, lay in a course of 3.45 mark 48.98 for the Hydrant Quadrant."

Smirk swung into action. "Punch it up to Warped ten!" he ordered. "We've got to beat them there!"

Beverage bounded over to Dacron and pulled him to his feet. She dragged the befuddled android to the Crewmover while apologizing to Capt. Smirk. "I-I thought I had him fixed, b-b-but . . . " she babbled, "there must still be something wrong with his software. I'll take him to Sick Bay and—uh—run a cleanup utility program on him."

"Just get him off my Bridge," Smirk raged.

"I think you should know, sir, that I—" Dacron began, but Beverage clamped a hand over his mouth and shoved him into the Crewmover before he could spill his guts.

After the doors closed, Bev sighed with relief and gave the Crewmover their destination: "Shipping and Receiving."

Dacron looked puzzled. "Doctor, you told the captain we were going to Sick Bay," he reminded her.

Bev shook her head. "We've got to be ready to UltraFax down to the Fountain of Youth as soon as our ship arrives at the planet," she said. "Do you think Captain Smirk would send you on another away mission after what just happened? If we're lucky, you and I can get down to the fountain before he knows we're leaving. Then it's up to you to state your case to Deanna."

Both ships raced at top speed toward the Hydrant Quadrant. In the midst of the chase, Capt. Smirk suddenly stood and turned to Westerly Flusher at the Tactical station.

"Mr. Flusher, secure a private channel to Deanna Troit on Ricardo's ship. Patch it through to my Ready Room,"

Smirk ordered, striding to the Ready Room door.

Once inside, Smirk turned on his desktop monitor, and Troit's image appeared. She stood in front of the huge pulsing engine on Ricardo's ship. Her arms were crossed, and she impatiently tapped the fingers of one hand against her arm. "Yes, Captain, what is it?" she asked curtly. "I'm very busy right now."

"Ah, yes. I'm sure you are," said Smirk, giving her his oiliest smile. "We've all been so busy lately, haven't we? But sometimes it's good to stop and smell the roses."

Troit frowned harder. "Get to the point," she snapped.

"Well, you're probably thinking that I've been so involved with this mission that I hadn't taken time to write to you lately," Smirk continued in his most buttery tone. "But now it can be told: I *couldn't* write to you. Starfreak orders, you know."

A shadow of doubt passed over Troit's cross expression. "Starfreak orders? But you're not in Starfreak anymore."

Smirk gave a debonair chuckle. "Yes, that's what everybody's supposed to think, isn't it?" he said with a wink, as if acknowledging a foolish charade they all had to maintain. Troit looked even more confused.

"Our cover has been working," Smirk continued. "Everybody in the galaxy disregards us because they think we're washed up. Meanwhile, we're hot on the trail of the Romanumens, on a top-secret mission—so top secret, in fact, that we couldn't break radio silence."

"Oh," said the bewildered Troit, who seemed to be debating whether or not to accept his story.

"And that's why I couldn't correspond with you anymore, my dear," Smirk said, "much as I yearned to do. I simply couldn't risk giving away the position of our ship. Especially since we were barely clinging to survival, doing without Starfreak support and supplies—all to intensify the illusion, naturally."

Smirk sighed deeply, as if the struggle had taken its toll. "Yes, we've given it our all," he said. "Yet I fear that in my zeal to perform my duty, I have risked the thing I cherish most: our romance. You must be quite angry with me for not contacting you—even though any communication between us in the last few days might have eventually led to the downfall of the federation."

"Well, I—" Troit said, reluctant to be cast in such a petulant light.

Smirk pressed on. "Dearest Deanna, would you deny me this chance, merely because I have also done my duty as a Starfreak officer? I still have a lifetime's worth of love poetry stored up for you, and soon there will be nothing between us. Just say you'll be mine."

Troit shook her head. "I don't know," she answered. "It's all so confusing."

"Just think about my words of love in the letters I sent," Smirk half-whispered, "and how much they moved you."

Troit got a faraway look in her eyes. "Yes," she admitted, "those letters did make me feel there was genuine sensitivity somewhere inside you. Although I must say that my empathic powers can't seem to pick it up from you right now."

"It's probably this darned communicator. We must have a bad connection," Smirk reasoned. "But surely you remember the poetry and outpourings of love I've written."

Troit blushed. "Yes, I do. I've even memorized some of them. They make me feel that our romance is . . . predestined, somehow. Those letters did touch something deep inside me, and it would be a shame to lose that feeling."

"Wonderful," Smirk said in an awestruck tone. He leaned forward and continued urgently, "Deanna, for once, listen to your heart, not your head. Say you'll marry me. This time we'll make it all the way through our engagement, I promise."

"Well . . . " Troit was still hesitant.

"Say yes," Smirk urged her. "It won't be binding. You know that federation law allows a three-day cooling-off period on any marriage proposal accepted over the communicator, as long as you notify your fiancé in writing if you decide to break it off."

Troit, deep in thought, ran her hand through her hair distractedly. Then she tossed her head, smiled and answered, "All right. I accept. You must have grown up a lot since we last broke up, or you couldn't have written those marvelous letters."

Smirk gave her his patented "stun" gaze and replied, "Just hold that thought, my darling, till we meet again." He blew a kiss at the communicator screen before switching it off.

The Mushy
Part

THE TWO STARSHIPS arrived simultaneously at the Hydrant Quadrant planet where the Fountain of Youth was located. They skidded to a halt, then hovered in orbit.

As soon as Capt. Smirk's ship was in position, UltraFax Chief O'Brine sent Bev and Dacron down to the Fountain of Youth.

Meanwhile, on Capt. Ricardo's ship, Guano, Troit and Smock stood on their Shipping platform and watched Checkout fiddle with the UltraFax controls. He checked the monitor and muttered, "Dere is already someone down dere."

"It might be someone from Captain Smirk's crew," said Guano, looking out the window at Smirk's ship, parked next to theirs. "They've caught up to us again."

"I'm sure *their* transporter chief, Mr. O'Brine, knows what he's doing," Troit said pointedly. "Why don't you just Fax us to the same spot? It's probably near the Fountain of Youth."

"I vas just about to do dat," Checkout said through clenched teeth. He energized the trio, sending them down to the coordinates occupied by Smirk's Away Team.

The Away Teams collided next to the fountain. Troit landed on top of Dacron; Smock materialized so close to

Bev that she could smell the Sen-Sen on his breath; and
Guano landed between the two couples. Swiftly they all
unscrambled themselves and stood up.

Bev and Smock stared at each other for a moment. Then
they both began speaking at once, interrupting each other
and starting anew in mid-thought as they sorted out what
had happened since their last phone call.

"I thought I would never see you again—"

"We have got a lot to talk about—"

"I haven't been able to stop thinking about you—"

"Why didn't I hear from you—"

"Our communicator could only receive messages, not
send them—"

Within moments, they were embracing, gazing into each
other's eyes, and murmuring highly technical, scientifi-
cally-correct endearments.

"Ugh! How mushy," Guano grumbled. She turned away
and hightailed it over to the fountain.

Troit also turned away, to give the lovers some privacy,
and found herself face-to-face with Dacron. He looked as
if he'd been watching her all along.

"Dacron," she murmured, disconcerted.

"Counselor Troit," he said. "Or rather, Chief Engineer
Troit. Or may I call you Deanna?"

"You may," she answered. She studied him for a moment, then ventured, "Dacron, I'm sensing strong feelings
of affection in you. Are you still under the influence of
your fall into the Fountain of Love?"

"Yes, I am," he said, shyly taking both her hands in his.
"The affection I feel is for you, Deanna."

Gently she pulled away. "Dacron, that's sweet," she told
him, "but you really shouldn't say any more. You see, I've
just become engaged to Captain Smirk."

Dacron stared at her, dumbstruck.

"He proposed over the communicator just a little while
ago, and I said yes," Troit continued.

The old Dacron would have made a gentlemanly retreat

upon hearing this news, but the new Dacron, saturated with Fountain of Truth water, could not keep silent.

"But Captain Smirk does not love you the way I do," Dacron protested. "He is only interested in you because you are unattainable. There is no depth to his feelings."

"That's what I thought," Troit responded, "until I read his letters. They show a completely different side of him: thoughtful, sensitive, caring, and even mature. I've come to love him through his correspondence."

"But *I* wrote those letters," Dacron blurted out.

"What?" Troit took a step back, astonished at the very idea.

"If you love the person revealed in this correspondence, Deanna, then it is me you love, not Captain Smirk," Dacron told her.

Troit shook her head. "Dacron, how can you expect me to believe that?" she chided him. "You may have developed some capacity for emotion, but you couldn't have written those letters. They were masterpieces. They showed a true depth of feeling."

"I wrote them all," Dacron insisted. "I can quote them. For instance, the one written on Stardate 44438.2 began: 'Dearest Deanna, As the moons of Frippery—4 cast their shadows over my pillow, I toss and turn, dreaming of your smile . . .' "

Troit gasped. "You've been reading the letters Captain Smirk wrote to me!" Without thinking, she slapped Dacron's face.

Tears filled Dacron's eyes—tears that contained a high Mountain Dew/H_2O ratio—and a single teardrop ran down his cheek. Still, the compulsion to tell everything would not let him give up. "The words were mine," he said, his tone subdued yet firm. "I signed Captain Smirk's name to them because we agreed I would ghostwrite for him. But I sincerely meant everything I wrote. It was the only way I could safely express my love for you."

"Why are you saying this?" Troit demanded with a catch

Without thnking, she slapped Dacron's face.

in her voice. She looked nearly as miserable as he did.

"Deanna." Dacron ventured to touch her shoulder, and when she did not resist, he went on, "If I were lying, your Betavoid powers would tell you so, would they not?"

Troit didn't answer, but her expression plainly revealed her inner turmoil. Dacron pressed on. "I can prove that I wrote those letters," he offered. "I shall challenge Captain Smirk to a duel. A poetry duel."

This novel suggestion made Troit smile in spite of herself. Emboldened, Dacron continued, "It will take place right now, while you and I are down here, so Captain Smirk cannot interfere with the outcome. Each of us will compose an impromptu poem for you. Then you will know that only I was capable of writing the letters which won your heart."

Troit nodded in agreement. "All right."

Dacron touched the communicator insignia on his chest. "Dacron to Captain Smirk."

"Go ahead, Dacron," came Smirk's voice.

"Captain, I am here on the surface of the planet with Deanna Troit—"

"What?!" Smirk screamed. Dacron and Troit cringed; even over the cheap, tinny speaker of the insignia, Smirk's voice packed a wallop. "You're supposed to be in Sick Bay," Smirk yelled.

"I UltraFaxed here to tell Deanna the truth about our correspondence," Dacron continued.

"You WHAT?!" Smirk hollered, his voice so loud that the insignia on Dacron's chest actually vibrated.

Dacron flicked the "reset" button behind his earlobe to restore his hearing, which had shut down automatically during the second of Smirk's high-decibel outbursts.

Dacron continued, "Deanna has agreed that if we each ad lib a poem, the results will confirm the actual author of the letters."

"That's ridiculous!" Smirk stormed. "Deanna, I shouldn't have to prove myself after all this time."

"You sound a little like your old slippery self, Captain,"

Troit said. "Aren't you up to the challenge?"

"But..." Smirk said. He paused for several moments, then continued, "Oh, all right. Just one poem? That won't be too hard. Not after all those other poems I've written. Should be a snap."

"Would you like to go first, Captain?" Dacron offered.

"No, thanks," Smirk answered quickly. "After you, Dacron."

"Very well," said Dacron. He thought for a minute, then turned and spoke to Deanna. "The secret garden of your heart / Is where I long to bloom and grow / So wilt thou let my spirit rest / Within the shelter of your soul?"

"Beautiful," Troit whispered, gazing into his eyes.

"What kind of poem is that?" came Smirk's gripe from the insignia speaker. "It doesn't even rhyme very well. 'Grow' and 'soul'?"

Troit swallowed hard and brushed away a tear. "Your turn, Captain Smirk," she said briskly.

"Oh-*kay!*" he responded heartily. "Here goes: Roses are red / Violets are blue / I like french kissing / How about you?"

There was a long pause. Finally Smirk prompted, "Well, what do you think? Kinda makes you feel hot all over, doesn't it?"

Troit didn't answer. She and Dacron were in the midst of a long and passionate kiss.

Watching them from nearby, Guano made a face and mumbled, "More mushy stuff." She flicked her insignia. "Guano to Checkout."

"Checkout here," came his voice from aboard Ricardo's ship.

"Fax me back there, will ya?" she demanded. "Oh, and I'm bringing along some souvenirs, so lock onto them and bring them up, too."

A third ship, undetected by the others, hovered in orbit far above the Fountain of Youth. It was the Romanumen flagship, lurking behind its croaking device.

"Sensors show four life forms and an android on the surface of the planet," reported the Romanumen first officer from his station on the Bridge of the wartbird. Then he stated, "Correction—three life forms. The fourth person just returned to one of their vessels. Those who remain are at the edge of the Fountain of Youth."

"What are they doing?" demanded the Romanumen captain. "Have they claimed the fountain yet by planting the Starfreak flag?"

"No, sir," said the first officer. "Sensors show they are . . ."—his lip curled in disgust—". . . kissing."

"Kissing?" The captain's tone was icy with disdain. "The discipline of Starfreak officers declines each time we encounter them. Let us take advantage of the situation while we can. Send down an Away Team with the Romanumen flag, and have them place it in the center of the fountain."

"Yes, sir," the first officer responded.

"Arm futon torpedoes!" the captain ordered. "Aim them at the orbiting ships. We will show them who rules this sector."

"Futon torpedoes armed and ready," announced the tactical officer. She flicked the switch that disabled the croaking device so the weapons system could fire.

Down on the planet, Bev came up for air after a long kiss with Smock and happened to glance at the sky just as the Romanumen ship uncroaked. "Aaaiiieee!" Bev screeched. The others looked where she was pointing and saw the Romanumen ship floating next to their own vessels.

Instantly Dacron flicked his communicator insignia. "Mr. O'Brine, four to Fax immediately to the Bridge," he ordered.

O'Brine had been napping at the UltraFax controls. Awakened by Dacron's order, he dazedly energized the Fax, accidentally engaging a mode designed to switch the positions of the Faxees.

When the two couples materialized on the Bridge of Smirk's ship, they found their partners switched: Dr. Flusher was embracing Troit, and Dacron was smooching with Smock. Hastily they disengaged and looked around the Bridge.

In response to the sudden appearance of the Romanumens, a Red Alert was already in progress; scarlet lights flashed on and off, and crewmembers dashed around aimlessly, scattering paperwork. Capt. Smirk was blow-drying his hair to prepare for battle.

Dacron ran to his Oops station, flung aside the ensign who'd temporarily taken his place, and opened a channel to Ricardo's ship. "Dacron to Captain Ricardo," he said. "There is a Romanumen wartbird uncroaking off your starboard bow. Suggest you take evasive action."

"I see it," Ricardo responded crabbily. "Just because I'm older than you, don't assume there's anything wrong with my eyesight."

"Yes sir," Dacron said, adding, "Captain, they have armed their futon torpedoes."

"I need Mr. Smock over here for tactical advice," Ricardo said. They heard Ricardo page Checkout and demand him to UltraFax Mr. Smock back to their ship. Ricardo lowered his shields for a moment to allow for the Faxing.

Smock gave Beverage a jaunty salute and told her, "Till we meet again." Then he disappeared amidst the sparkles of an UltraFax beam.

"Sir," said Dacron, turning to Capt. Smirk, "I suggest we take evasive action."

Smirk was staring at Troit. "No," he answered Dacron without turning his gaze from Troit. "If Ricardo is going to stand and fight, so are we."

Huge explosions rocked both ships simultaneously. The Romanumens had fired their first round of futon torpedoes.

"Damage report!" Smirk demanded, striking a macho pose in the center of the Bridge.

When the two couples materialized, they found their partners switched.

"Decompression on Decks 23 and 76," said Westerly, checking the sensors. "Deck 72 is missing. It's snowing on Decks 39 and 40, and there's a six-inch base and two inches of new powder on Deck 41."

Troit glared back at Smirk. "If you think you're going to impress me by risking our necks in some cowboy stunt, you're wrong," she declared. "I know what you tried to pull off with those letters Dacron wrote for you, and I think it's despicable."

She touched her communicator insignia. "Troit to Captain Ricardo. Permission to Fax aboard, sir."

"Granted," responded Ricardo.

Troit turned toward Dacron. "I'll see you later," she told him.

After Troit Faxed away, a second Romanumen torpedo hit Smirk's ship. Upon impact, the crew shifted to one side on cue, more or less simultaneously, and then regained their balance.

"Damage report!" Smirk demanded again.

"Deck 72 has turned up in the Lost and Found on HolidayDeck 3," Westerly reported. "There's an ozone alert on Decks 56 and 68. A flock of sheep has gotten loose on Deck 97."

"Captain," said Dacron, consulting his console, "the Romanumens are powering up their futon torpedoes again. Our shields will not withstand another blow."

Still Smirk held his ground, reluctant to surrender this chance to play the hero.

Over on Ricardo's ship, meanwhile, the computer was getting peeved about the danger they faced.

"Why I got mixed up in this, heaven knows," said the computer's voice, which by now they all knew belonged to Woksauna Troit. "I should have left while I had the chance."

"Mother, it's a little late to have regrets about hiding on board our ship," Troit pointed out.

"It's never too late for regret, spittle one," Woksauna retorted.

"Computer, report the condition of the Romanumen weapon systems," Mr. Smock ordered.

"A third array of futon torpedoes is being armed. Their countdown gives sixty seconds to impact. Shields will not withstand another strike," Woksauna stated in her matter-of-fact computer voice. Then, shifting to her own personal shrill tone, she continued, "Speaking of regret, Deanna, if you'd have taken my advice you'd be married by now, and at least I could have seen some grandchildren before I died.

"After all I've—" Woksauna interrupted herself and switched to her computer voice: *"Forty-five seconds to impact."* Then she resumed harping: "—done for you, the least you could do would be to settle down, get married, have children, and suffer like the rest of us."

"Captain Smirk," said Ricardo over the "hey, you" frequency, "we have determined that our shields cannot stand another strike from the Romanumen torpedoes. And our sensors show that the Romanumens have already placed their claim on the fountain. I think both of our ships should withdraw."

"Twenty seconds to impact," said Woksauna the computer. "But would you listen to your mother, Deanna? Of course not. You thought you were too smart to—"

She interrupted herself to speak as the computer again. *"Ten seconds. Nine, eight, seven—*Oh, nuts*—five, four—"*

"All right!" Smirk reluctantly conceded over the communication channel. "Let's get out of here."

Both ships kicked into Warped drive just as the Romanumens fired their third deadly volley of futon torpedoes.

"The Romanumens have already placed their claim on
the fountain."

9

Guano's
Hat Trick

"**P**SSST! DACRON!"

Dacron turned around and saw that Georgie, sitting directly behind him, was passing him a note. The sheet of lined notebook paper had been folded into a self-sealing triangle. Dacron opened it, moving slowly so as not to catch the eye of Admiral Nonsequitur.

At the front of the room, Nonsequitur paced back and forth, deeply involved in his ranting and raving. Somehow he'd managed to keep his mind on the same subject for more than a minute. He was well into the third hour of scolding the crews of both ships, who sat in rows before him, squished into uncomfortable classroom-style chairs. This was Starfreak headquarters' lecture hall, designed specifically for occasions when the brass wanted to intimidate the rank-and-file.

At first, the crews of Ricardo and Smirk had cowered as Nonsequitur screamed at them for allowing the Romanumens to capture the Fountain of Youth. Nonsequitur ignored the fact that they'd managed to escape without injuries or major damage to their ships. Instead, he piled on the guilt over Starfreak's tremendous loss of potential income from the fountain.

Everybody was duly penitent—for a while. But they discovered that you can only cringe for so long before the cringe reflex wears out. By about the middle of the second hour, most of the crewmembers had realized that the worst was over: Starfreak was taking away their jobs and their ships, and nothing more could be done about it, so why worry?

They'd begun tapping their fingers, whispering among themselves, shooting spitballs, and passing notes, such as the one Dacron had just received:

Dacron,
　　What are you going to do with yourself now that we're out of Starfreak for good?
　　　　　　　　　　　　　　　　　　　　　　Georgie

Dacron pulled out a mechanical pencil and composed an answer in his methodical, precise script:

Georgie:
　　I have been invited to assume a position with the staff of Ready Reference. They welcome my input, since I can answer most patrons' questions merely by consulting my memory banks. This leaves the reference books free for others to use.
　　Deanna Troit will accompany me. She will seek employment within the counseling field in the Greater Milwaukee area.
　　　　　　　　　　　　　　　　　　　　　　Dacron

Others whispered back and forth about their own plans. Smock and Beverage intended to stay together; he'd already proposed, asking her to be his significant other. Piker wanted to open his own restaurant, specializing in Kringle cuisine. Checkout, realizing he was unemployable outside of Starfreak, was hoping to enroll in graduate school.

Up at the front of the room, Nonsequitur paused to sip from the glass of water at his podium. Then he declared to the group, "If Starfreak auctions off both your ships,

Piker wanted to open his own restaurant, specializing in Kringle cuisine.

we might scrape up enough money to pay for this year's executive board retreat at a luxury resort. And speaking of the auction, we'll need to sell your uniforms, too. Leave them here today when I dismiss you.

"Now," he continued, "let me tell you the worst thing about this whole botched affair. Starfreak learned this morning that the Romanumens don't intend to sell any of the Fountain of Youth water. They're going to hoard it all for themselves. So the rest of us in the federation won't have access to it at all."

Guano, sitting near the front row, was one of the few who were still half-listening to Nonsequitur. When she heard this remark, she suddenly perked up and raised her hand.

"What is it?" Nonsequitur said.

"Admiral," said Guano, "if the Romanumens are hoarding the water, that makes it especially valuable, doesn't it?"

"Of course it does," growled Nonsequitur. "It's the old law of supply and command."

"So if someone besides the Romanumens has water from the Fountain of Youth, they'd be sitting on a fortune," Guano suggested.

"Yes, yes, of course—but no one else has any," Nonsequitur replied irritably.

"Suppose Starfreak could get their hands on some?" Guano continued coyly. "Say . . . if a certain crewmember knew where there was a good supply of it?"

As Guano went on, others in the room began to realize that something significant was happening, and they suspended their note-passing, whispering and flirting to listen to her.

"Do you think that if that crewmember turned the water over to Starfreak for future sales, the High Command would agree to use some of the profit to reinstate both USS *Endocrine*s and their crews?" asked Guano. "Do you think you could get us a signed contract to that effect? A contract stating that once this crewmember turns over, say, thirteen half-barrels of Fountain of Youth water, both ships will be put back in service immediately?"

Nonsequitur stood and stared at Guano, absorbing this information. He stood there for a good five minutes, until Guano began to wonder if his brain had finally been overloaded past the point of no return.

Finally he blurted, "Let me find out for you," turned on his heel, and headed out of the lecture hall. The room buzzed with excited conversation as the crews speculated on their chances of reinstatement.

UltraFax Chief Checkout leaned over and asked Guano, "Does dis have anyting to do with dose barrels you had me Fax up to da ship on your last avay mission?"

Guano gave him a condescending smile. "Gee, Checkout, how did you ever guess?"

After a long time Nonsequitur came back, holding an official-looking document. It spelled out Guano's terms, and it had been signed by Starfreak's head honchos. Guano asked the two captains to check the legitimacy of the signatures to make sure the signers had authority.

"They're big shots, all right," said Capt. Smirk.

Capt. Ricardo agreed. "Those are the same signatures that appear on our paychecks. I'd recognize them anywhere." After the captains signed the document, Guano gave Admiral Nonsequitur the coordinates on board Capt. Ricardo's *Endocrine* where Starfreak would find its barrels of Fountain of Youth water.

"Hmmph. Looks like you got out of this one," Nonsequitur grumbled. "Both ships are back in commission, and you all have your old jobs back."

Everybody cheered.

That evening, they all gathered in the Ten-Foreplay lounge of Capt. Ricardo's ship to celebrate. In honor of the occasion, Guano declared that drinks were on the house. She even broke out her supply of water from the fountains.

Mr. Snot, sitting at the bar, took several gulps of his drink. "It was good o' you to hold a little o' this Fountain o' Youth water in reserve from the barrels you turned over to Starfreak," he told Guano, holding out his glass for a refill.

Guano refilled his glass and turned away, muttering to herself, "I knew some people around here desperately needed it." She was being unusually polite this evening because she'd been guzzling Fountain of Love water with a vengeance.

Snot clinked his glass against Dr. McCaw's and Yoohoo's, proposing a toast: "Here's to our return to a civilized ship."

"Here, here," McCaw rasped. "One where everyone knows their job, yet isn't required to do it."

" 'Hey, you' frequencies open, sir," Yoohoo added irrelevantly; she was already practicing her usual routine.

Checkout reached over to attempt to clink his glass against theirs, but nobody noticed, so he simply shrugged and kept on drinking.

Zulu, sitting at a table in the center of Ten-Foreplay, wasn't quite as happy to be returning to the status quo. "I rather enjoyed our status as outcasts," he told Georgie and Westerly, who sat with him. "It was a challenge to be running lean and mean."

"Too much of a challenge, if you ask me," Georgie responded. "I felt like an idiot when all the systems went down at once and Dacron had to bail us out. There's nothing worse for an engineer's ego than having an android come to the rescue."

"I could have saved the day instead, if you'd have let me," Westerly offered.

"Hmmm. I guess there *is* something worse, after all," said Georgie, brightening up. "Thanks, Westerly."

Westerly stared at Georgie for a moment, trying to determine whether or not he was being sarcastic. But Georgie's expression was unreadable thanks to the visor which hid his eyes, so Westerly turned his attention back to the banana split he was eating.

"Speaking of Dacron, where is he?" Zulu asked. "I thought *everybody* was coming to this party."

"He and Deanna Troit made a token appearance," Georgie said. "Then they left for some . . . uh . . . privacy." He gave Zulu a knowing smirk. "Dacron wants to demonstrate to Deanna that he's—" Georgie hesitated, glancing at Westerly, then spelled out, "F-U-L-L-Y F-U-N-C-T-I-O-N-A-L."

Westerly protested around a mouthful of banana split, "Hey, no fair. You know I haven't taken Introductory Spelling yet at the Academy."

Zulu told Georgie, "I guess that explains why Beverage Flusher and Mr. Smock didn't stay long either, huh?"

"Yeah," said Georgie. "They're probably over in the lab, testing out some new theorems." Zulu and Georgie burst into raucous laughter while Westerly toyed with the cherry atop his banana split, debating whether to eat it or throw it across the room to start a food fight.

At a nearby table, Capt. Ricardo sipped his Earl Grape tea, then asked, "Well, what insights have the two of you gained from the new assignments you'd held?"

Wart, mindful that he was speaking to the captain, tried to put it as diplomatically as he could. "I have a new appreciation for the skill required of the ship's counselor," he stated. "Managing human emotion is a complex task." Capt. Ricardo nodded approvingly and glanced away. Wart added under his breath, "Mostly because humans are a bunch of sniveling crybabies."

"And what have you learned, Number 1?" Ricardo asked Piker.

"Plenty," Piker said, shaking his head in awe. "The human body is such an intricate system of diverse organs. The amount of knowledge a medical doctor needs is incredibly humbling. Toward the end there, I even resorted to getting advice from the medical staff and the reference books instead of just guessing."

"Mmmmm...yes," Ricardo responded. "Well, it certainly will be much better having you both back in your own jobs again."

Way over in a dark corner of Ten-Foreplay, a solitary figure sat in the shadows, chin in hand. It was Capt. Smirk. He held up a piece of paper and read it for the umpteenth time that evening:

Starfreak Official Form No. 432-A–6699
Official Disengagement Notice

Notice is hereby given that the undersigned wishes to break off an engagement to be married, pursuant to Article 3322 of the Official Starfreak Code, which allows the cancellation of any marriage proposal made and/or accepted via a starship communication device, provided such notice is given within three (3) working days, and in consideration of which, time is of the essence, the early bird gets the worm, etc. etc., so get a move on, eh?

Signed: *Deanna Troit*
Stardate: 44453.7

Witness: DACRON
Stardate: 44453.7

Smirk felt an especially sharp pang at seeing Dacron's signature on the document—Dacron, his erstwhile right-hand man and secret rival, who now possessed the affections of the woman Smirk himself coveted.

Smirk knew that asking one's latest lover to sign as the witness to the disengagement document was a pretty well-established custom. Heaven knows, he'd done it himself often enough. Yet being on the receiving end was a bitter blow.

Smirk shook his head, then crumpled the document in his fist. *I've had it with women,* he decided. *If I can't have*

Deanna, I don't want anybody. I'll go through life a sol-
itary man. I'll drift around in space till the end of my
days, a model of chastity and self-control—my life a tes-
tament to this matchless love that is now lost forever.

Smirk heard a rustle at his side and turned to see a Ten-
Foreplay cocktail waitress standing next to the table. "Can
I get you something, sir?" she asked.

Smirk gave her the once-over, then smiled with approval. "You certainly can," he said. "Bring me a magnum
of that Fountain of Love water . . . and two glasses."

"Oh," the waitress remarked pleasantly, "will Counselor
Troit be joining you?"

"Who?" Smirk responded.

"Counselor Deanna Troit. I heard the two of you were
engaged," said the waitress.

"Oh, *her*. No, that's all over," Smirk said breezily. "No,
my dear, the second glass is for you. I was about to ask if
you would join me." The waitress blushed with pleasure,
and Smirk added, "What's a classy dame like you doing in
a watered-down watering hole like this?"

Boldly go where nobody ever wanted to go before!

Leah Rewolinski's *Star Wreck* books—which parody everyone's favorite endlessly rerun TV series, not to mention
everyone's favorite interminable number of movie sequels
and everyone's favorite "next generation" spin-off—are
turning the world—and the galaxy—on its collective pointed
ear!

STAR WRECK: THE GENERATION GAP
_____ 92802-5 $3.99 U.S./$4.99 CAN.

STAR WRECK II: THE ATTACK OF THE JARGONITES
_____ 92737-1 $3.99 U.S./$4.99 CAN.

STAR WRECK III: TIME WARPED
_____ 92891-2 $3.99 U.S./$4.99 CAN.

STAR WRECK IV: LIVE LONG AND PROFIT
_____ 92985-4 $3.99 U.S./$4.99 CAN.

Coming in September
STAR WRECK V: THE UNDISCOVERED
NURSING HOME